THE BURNING BOYS

John Fuller has written four novels, including the Whitbread Award-winning *Flying to Nowhere*, and two collections of short stories. He is also the author of twelve collections of poetry, the latest of which, *Stones and Fires* won the 1996 Forward Poetry Prize. His new novel, *A Skin Diary*, is published by Chatto & Windus.

BY JOHN FULLER

Poetry

Fairground Music
The Tree That Walked
Cannibals and Missionaries
Epistles To Several Persons
The Mountain In The Sea
Lies And Secrets
The Illusionists
Waiting For The Music
The Beautiful Inventions
Selected Poems 1954 to 1982
Partingtime Hall (with James Fenton)
The Grey Among The Green
The Mechanical Body
Stones And Fires
Collected Poems

Fiction

Flying To Nowhere
The Adventures of Speedfall
Tell It Me Again
The Burning Boys
Look Twice
The Worm And The Star
A Skin Diary

Criticism

A Reader's Guide To W.H. Auden
The Sonnet

For Children

Herod Do Your Worst
Squeaking Crust
The Spider Monkey Uncle King
The Last Bid
The Extraordinary Wood Mill And Other Stories
Come Aboard And Sail Away

Editor

The Vintage Book Of Love Poetry
The Dramatic Works Of John Gay

John Fuller

THE BURNING BOYS

VINTAGE

Published by Vintage 1991

3 5 7 9 10 8 6 4 2

First published by Chatto & Windus Ltd, 1989

Vintage Books
Random House UK Limited
20 Vauxhall Bridge Road, London SW1V 2SA

Random House Australia (Pty) Limited
20 Alfred Street, Milsons Point, Sydney
New South Wales 2061, Australia

Random House New Zealand Limited
18 Poland Road, Glenfield, Auckland 10, New Zealand

Random House South Africa (Pty) Limited
Endulini, 5a Jubilee Road, Parktown 2193, South Africa

Random House UK Limited Reg. No. 954009

ISBN 0 09 974850 9

Papers used by Random House UK Limited
are natural, recyclable products made from wood grown in
sustainable forests. The manufacturing processes conform to
the environmental regulations of the country of origin

Printed and bound in Great Britain by
Cox & Wyman Ltd, Reading, Berkshire

1

The alley had no name. It bent slightly in the middle so that you could not see from one end to the other. The high brick walls were the sides of houses pretending to have nothing to do with it, except for one green gate that David had never seen opened. He had once tried the latch, but the gate wouldn't move. It could have been glued shut.

When David came home from school he would pretend that the journey might continue unpredictably beyond the entrance to the alley. He might walk to the corner of Mayfield Road, and on up Mayfield Road to Bennet Avenue where the houses stood by themselves, some-times half-hidden by trees. He could, if he wanted to, walk right to the end of Bennet Avenue where the Witch lived. But he usually entered the alley.

Once when he was halfway through he had seen the Witch coming towards him from the other end. She seemed even taller than usual, walking unnaturally erect, almost leaning backwards, clutching her coat at the neck. He had turned and run out of the alley, round the corner and back up the road. At a safe distance he had waited in a gateway for the Witch to come out of the alley and away down towards Mayfield Road. But she had not gone towards Mayfield Road. She came out of the alley and turned instead towards him, walking stiffly and quickly, looking around her with little jerks of the head.

David had turned and run even further away down the road to school, stopping every now and then to see if the Witch was coming after him. When the road was clear he came back carefully, knowing that she was thin enough to be hiding behind a tree. He ran down the alley, and fell on the gravel, hurting his knee.

It seemed to him that you couldn't decide whether to be shocked or relieved at the sight of the little blossoming graze, with the beads of blood oozing out and the pieces of gravel sticking to it. It seemed in a way natural to have it there. Without it, the pain would be too mysterious.

He walked carefully out of the alley into the sunlight of Viewforth Road. The blood was trickling towards his sock. He decided to leave it, and to see if he could get home before it reached the sock. When he limped into the kitchen, Jean seized him by both shoulders.

'Look at you again!' she said, turning him round as though he were trying on a new jacket. 'You can't stay upright one minute, you can't.'

The blood had reached his sock. When he untied his garter and pulled down the overlapping part of the sock, the stained rim unfolded like a butterfly. Jean dabbed at the knee with a warm flannel.

'How am I going to get the gravel out?' she said.

'Leave it,' said David.

He was standing on one leg with the other stuck out across a kitchen chair, holding on to his aunt. He looked past her curls at the clock above the range, wondering if there was something he could eat to keep him going till tea. She smelled of soap.

6

'How can I leave it?' she replied. 'It'll go septic. Always in the wars, you are.'

It was true. It seemed almost as natural for him to have a scab on his knee as for a man to have a moustache. A scab was even quite like a moustache, a little square smudge like a Hitler moustache.

David had once appeared at the door of the lounge when Granny and Jean and Mrs Elswick had been sorting clothes for the Deaf and Dumb, wearing a Hitler moustache of Jean's mascara. Jean had killed herself laughing until she discovered what the moustache was made of.

'Little devil,' she complained. 'That cost me four-and-eleven at George and Taylor's.'

Granny didn't like him to pick his scabs.

'Can't you leave that knee alone,' she would say. 'It won't heal.'

But the scabs did heal, however much David would delay the process by detaching the dry margins of the area. He didn't know if there was greater pleasure in this gradual encroachment or in waiting until the whole scab could come off like a lid.

There was always some reason for a scab, though by the picking stage it was usually forgotten. This one was the Witch's fault, whether she knew about it or not. David thought that perhaps it might protect him from her, and for that reason he didn't pick it as much as he wanted to. He wore it as he might wear a little badge. When women rattled collecting boxes at you at street corners you bought a flag and then they left you alone. David knew that when his knee was healed he would meet the Witch again.

There was an old dog in the alley that used to walk to meet him. The whole of its back was like a scab, matted and dusty. When David talked to it, it looked up at him with a watery concern in its eye. When he dared to put his hand on its back with pretended fondness, the dog turned and padded away. The coat felt hard and hot, like a pie crust.

George Robinson's father had shut his son's hand in the car door and two of his fingers had come off. David wondered what those scabs had felt like, and what had happened to the fingers. They would have had scabs, too.

When he came out of the alley, Viewforth Road always seemed sunnier than any of the other streets. The row of houses on the left faced east, the row on the right faced west. His grandmother's house was Number 20, on the right. From his room in the attic you could see the sea, and in the evening when he got home from school the sun made the windows of the west-facing terrace blaze.

David thought that he was lucky to live on his side . the street. The houses were higher, and the little gardens deeper. Many of them had neat displays of lavender, geraniums, carnations, and gleaming white rocks like small Matterhorns. Mrs Thesiger lived on his side of the street.

The other side of the street was darker. The Dales never painted their house, and their son Ritchie was always making a noise with his motorbike. David was amazed at the size of the motorbike close to, but he was afraid to touch it. It seemed far too broad for anyone to get his legs across it and reach the pedals at the same time. With its great petrol tank it was like a dentist's chair mounted on a torpedo.

Ritchie Dale had once asked his aunt Jean out on it, though she hadn't gone. David had overheard her telling her friend Phyllis about it when he was playing under the green tassels of the table and they hadn't known he was there.

'I'm not opening my legs to get on that thing,' Jean had said. 'And not for any other reason either.'

'I wouldn't,' said Phyllis. 'He's a sly devil, that Ritchie Dale. You know what he did to Mabel Croft?'

8

David never discovered what Ritchie Dale had done to Mabel Croft, because Jean had crossed her legs at that moment (perhaps at the thought of opening them) and her toe had caught his shoulder.

'You little monkey!' she had exclaimed. 'Always hiding and listening in!'

'I wasn't listening,' said David. 'And I wasn't hiding. I was here already.'

'Come on, Phyllis,' said Jean. 'Let's go upstairs. We'll make a cup of tea and go upstairs.'

Jean was his mother's younger sister. She had taken him on when his mother had been killed by a bomb in the Blitz. David always thought that was a silly word. It sounded like a kind of cleaning powder. And he couldn't understand why everyone talked about it as though it were a single event, or if it was, how it could have happened to such a lot of people. He remembered a loud noise and the lampshade bouncing up towards the ceiling. That was when they were in London. They had seen his father off into the air force, but they had stayed in London. Mr Collinson had been very kind to his mother, and one day had taken him to the pictures and bought him a pear. He didn't know it was a bomb when the lampshade hit the ceiling, because he hadn't heard any air-raid warning and he was alone in bed, reading his comic. He knew then that he should have been in the cellar. Later he saw the firemen at the Collinson house, and everyone was standing in the street. He had put on his dressing-gown and slippers and gone into the street. His slippers crunched the broken glass. He knew that his mother had gone round to see the Collinsons. But when he saw what had happened to the Collinson house he did not know where his mother was.

Sometimes he could not remember those days. There 9

were parts of it that had stuck in his mind. His father shouting. There were toys he used to have that he had no longer: a red truck, large enough to sit on and move around with his feet, a Walt Disney book into which his mother had glued a piece of white felt to hold pins. The pins were needed for a game or puzzle included in the book, but David had forgotten what it was. It was something to do with Goofy. He often thought of the book, and felt it would be important to recollect the precise nature of the game. He thought of the book's big soft pages. He could picture Goofy's splayed fingers in gloves with the three converging pen strokes on their backs like incomplete arrows. But he could not remember the purpose of the pins.

For a time he had slept with his aunt, in her big bed with the shiny pink eiderdown. That was before his room in the attic was ready. It could not have been for long, perhaps no longer than a week, but David remembered it very well. He would be sent up before anyone else had begun to think of going to bed. Sometimes he went up when Jacko was still getting ready to go out, flattening his hair with two brushes, working them rapidly and alternately at each side and at the top. The hair stretched back from his forehead in black swathes, and he wiped away the tiny curtain of brilliantine at its margin with a towel.

'I'm off then,' he would shout.

'Where to?' Granny would ask.

'Out.'

Granny had left a glass of milk for David on the bedside table, and left the bedside lamp on, with its pink fringe. He would drink the milk, and then turn off the light. He would be asleep when Jean came up to bed, but would be half aware of her moving around the room, taking off her things and opening and shutting drawers. The wardrobe was on his side of the bed, and if he opened one eye he

10

might see her stockinged legs as she stood in front of it hanging up her dress. Sometimes her feet might be bare, as they were when she was on the beach. David somehow found this very strange, even though he walked about on the carpet with bare feet himself. He didn't dare to open the other eye as well, because Jean might then see that he was awake, and he did not know what else he might see. When her feet moved out of his range of vision he had no idea what she was doing. There were sounds of jar tops being unscrewed and sounds of rustling. The light in the room was strange because it came from her bedside lamp and not from his, and because it threw the shadow of activities he could not guess at.

He would doze off, only to be half aware later that she was lying beside him, warm and heavy. Her weight pressed down the mattress and tilted him towards the centre of the bed. It was like being in a cave, the slopes and boulders of her body relaxed yet protective, smelling of pink cardigans and bathwater. He didn't know why he found this so exciting. In what seemed like the middle of the night Jean would stir at the sound of Jacko's key in the front door and shift her position in the bed, sighing slightly. Sometimes her arm might reach out over David's chest, or a warm knee touch his bottom, sending strange prickles down his leg.

Jacko, who had refused to have David sharing his room on the grounds that it would prevent him from having his friends up there, was indignant when David was given the attic.

'I could have used it,' he said. 'Why couldn't I have had it?'

'I told you you could have it three years ago,' said Granny. 'You couldn't be bothered to clear it up.'

'David hasn't cleared it up.'

'Don't be daft, Jacko,' said Granny indignantly. 'Little David can't clear it up, can he?'

11

To David, he would say: 'You're a lucky bargee.'

And for a time he used to come up to the attic, and stand about with his hands in his pockets, turning over the corner of the rug with one toe. David would try to interest him in his Dinky toys, but Jacko was not interested. He might breathe on the window-pane, and write his name on it. Then he would go downstairs again, and David would be left in peace. In fact, Jacko was not often at home.

'I'm off out then,' he would call out from the hall.

'Where's out?' Granny would ask.

'Fred's,' he would reply.

David would rub out Jacko's name and look out across the rooftops to the sea. In the mornings it was flat, blueish and indistinct, but in the evenings grey, silvery and wrinkled. If he looked very hard he thought he could almost see the movement of the waves. It was like the scaly skin of a sleepy sea creature.

He liked being at the top of the house, even though it meant that he no longer shared Jean's bed. There was a low cupboard beneath the sloping ceiling on one side of the attic, and another on the opposite side. He could get in among the cases and the junk and feel that he could climb right round to the other side, but it was so dark that he was afraid to do it, and it was difficult to move. Granny called it junk, but to David it seemed like treasure. There was a box with parts of a machine which he could not fit together, a handle that revolved slowly with an agreeable whirring noise because of a pair of cog-wheels in its casing. There was a chest of knives and forks wrapped in tissue paper and stained rainbow-black. There was a broken rocking-horse which Granny had told Jacko to get out for him, but which Jacko had scornfully said he was too old for. There were several things made of khaki canvas, with straps and buckles and stencilled numbers. There was a large metal tank, very cold to the touch, that made little piddling sounds like the toilet. Pipes led to it, and away from it, that were wrapped in felt that smelled of plasticine. David had the idea that not only might he be able to get all round the attic through a maze of cupboards, but that he might also be able to find another room that nobody knew about, perhaps above his own room. Or maybe there was a hidden connection with the attic next door, and he could explore the whole length of Viewforth Road, boring holes through ceilings and being able to watch Sylvia Elswick having a bath or Mrs Thesiger sitting up in bed eating bacon and eggs off a tray, probably still wearing her fox furs.

He liked to find other places in the house to hide: under the table in the front room, behind the sink in the wash-house, in the cupboard under the stairs. But he couldn't hide in these places for long. The wash-house, with its tinny smell and damp stone, was too cold. There was no room in the cupboard under the stairs, and after he had once upset a shelf of tins and bottles and broken one of them, he was told not to go in there again. His favourite place was under the table, where he would retire with the wooden tub of brightly-coloured spills, weaving them into coloured mats which became roofs to shelter his Dinky toys. When he came home from school, emerging from the darkness of the alley into the bright terraces of Viewforth Road, with their familiar surfaces of orange brick-work and green paint, it was under the table in the front room that he most looked forward to being, reading his book or making a landscape in the cross-pieces of the table legs. Granny would come in and out with the tea things, laying out the protective pads that unfolded to fit the table exactly, taking the tablecloth out of the sideboard drawer and settling it over the table with a few easy motions of her 13 hands. David would hear things being placed on the table above him and guess what they were by the kind of noise they made: the tray with the teapot, a plate of bread and butter, a handful of spoons, forks and knives.

'I know you're there, David,' she would sing out, as she came and went with the tea things.

And he would keep quite still and silent, because it was part of the game. But really he wanted to find a hiding place that nobody knew about, where he could be quite alone and yet be aware of what was going on. And before long he found it: there was a long shallow cupboard in the kitchen, the topmost of a whole wall of cupboards, just beneath the ceiling and too high to be of use. Another reason why it wasn't used was because the wooden clothes-rack that worked on a pulley prevented the doors from opening when it was fully hoisted to the ceiling. David found it difficult to get up there. He had to lower the clothes-rack just enough for the cupboard doors to be opened, and then he had to climb up from a chair to the dresser and from the dresser to the top of the broom-cupboard door. The door had to be open to give him a foothold, and so it was a very uncertain foothold. He had to wedge a chair against the door before he began, and he had to trust that no one would notice the wedged chair and the lowered clothes rack once he had reached the cupboard and almost closed the doors in on himself.

The cupboard wasn't quite empty. It had some clean, possibly unused sheets in it, stiff linen that smelled of roses and dust, like his grandmother's room. But he could extend himself on these and pretend he was asleep on the ocean. It was like a little coffin.

One evening, when his grandmother was at the Deaf and Dumb, and Jacko was as usual out, he climbed up to the cupboard with a little torch and *Radio Fun*. Gert and

14

Daisy were landgirls outwitting a black-marketeer: in the last picture they foiled him by rolling him up in turf with their pitchforks. Round and round he went, unwinding a whole field. Worms waved from the outside of the enormous swiss roll of grass and soil, and his head and feet stuck out from either end. It was frightening to see the underneath of the field like that. It was like seeing someone's skin peeled back.

Jean and her friend Phyllis came into the kitchen to make themselves a pot of tea. They stoked the fire, and sat at the table with their elbows on it, holding their teacups with both hands. Phyllis, who had finished her training as a nurse, was still wearing her uniform. David liked to see the white collar against her olive skin, the bare arms, the accessories like the pin holding the starched cap and the upside-down watch on a fob with its own little pocket.

'Is everyone out then?' asked Phyllis.

'Yes, they're all out,' said Jean.

'What about David?'

'He's up in the attic.'

David thrilled to hear this. He knew that he should call out and say that he was not in the attic but there in the kitchen a few feet above their heads and could hear all that they were saying, but the moment passed when he could do it. They chatted on, and David turned back to his comic.

He was drowsy, and knew that he should have been in bed. He didn't really even listen to what they were saying because he didn't understand a lot of it, and what he did understand embarrassed him. Besides, they kept lowering their voices to a whisper, and Phyllis kept touching Jean's forearm, pushing it slightly as if to make her believe what she was saying, and then leaning back with a giggle.

He read his comic again and again. He kept it open at the same page. Gert had her hands on her hips. Daisy was still 15 holding her pitchfork, and pointing. Both of them had glee-ful smiles, and sharp edges to their blouses and trousers which were clean and unrumpled. The only sign that they had been digging was a smudge on Gert's right cheek. The enormous basket of eggs was quite safe. It stood by the farm gate to the left of the picture, in the company of three laughing hens, while the man with the moustache went on rolling down the hill, tightly imprisoned in the hot damp turf, with worms falling down his neck.

He realised that Jean and Phyllis had stopped talking, but he knew that they were still there because he could hear a clanking noise. He raised himself on one elbow to look through the crack in the cupboard doors and saw that they had brought the kitchen scales over to the table in front of them. Phyllis had unbuttoned the starched front of her uniform, and her brassiere lay unfastened across her neck like a tangled parachute. As she leaned forward, her breast nosed out of her blouse and swung free above the pan of the scales.

David was astonished. He imagined at first that she had hurt herself. Why else whould anyone start to remove their clothes? He remembered Great Uncle Alfred when he thought he'd been stung by a wasp, pulling his shirt out of his trousers and turning round like a dog chasing its tail. Aunt Bea had had to look for the place on his ribs where the sting was supposed to be, with Alfred holding up the scroll of shirt and not minding that everyone could see. But this was different. David had never seen a breast before, or did not think that he had. He knew that they particularly belonged in their place, and were heavily armoured for that reason.

'Ooh, it's cold!' said Phyllis, as she lowered her breast on to the pan. What had seemed to be of almost liquid shape as it swayed above the metal settled plumply, the nipple appearing to seal or secure the mysteriously volatile contents. She put one of the hexagonal cast iron weights on the scales.

'Yes!' she cheered. The weight had not descended. She added another. 'Thirteen ounces.'

David was reminded of the butcher's. Was she going to cut it off?

Then it was his aunt's turn.

His aunt's breast was larger, whiter, bluer, blunter. It needed the pound weight and two smaller ones.

'You're leaning on it,' said Phyllis.

'No, I'm not,' said Jean indignantly.

They compared their breasts in shape and size, bunching them up in their cupped hands. David felt the blood thudding in his head and neck. What had at first seemed to be a bizarre experiment, the consequence of a bet, was becoming more certainly something secret that he was never intended to witness. And yet it was of supreme interest. In a curious way, although they did not know he was there, it was as though only he could fully appreciate the exhibition, or as though he were intended to take part in it. His body was alerted, drained, unfulfilled. His heart was beating quickly. When Phyllis admiringly traced her finger down the contours of his aunt's bosom, encircling the nipple on the way, leaving it standing out sturdily like the worn end of a lipstick, he was not sure that it was not himself doing it, so intense was his involvement.

And yet he remained hidden in his cupboard, the forgotten torch shining askance on the black and white windows of his comic. He was as distant from the spectacle below him as a theatre audience, and yet wrought to the nervous pitch of a performer waiting to make his entrance. But his role had not yet been written.

2

In the seconds before impact, all he could think of was the absurdity of it. All the distance travelled, all the dangers, the willed effort, the sense of being counted on, the waiting, the routine. All the missions, however precariously achieved. The skills acquired at first for no certain purpose, long ago, then wonderfully finding their fulfilment.

The mountain shouldn't have been there. It wasn't meant to be there at all. He should have been hundreds of feet above the highest mountain for miles. But there was no time to wonder what had gone wrong with his instruments. He couldn't even remember when he last looked at any of his instruments. The journey itself was ridiculous, in any case. Why should a crack fighter pilot be required to deliver from Llandwrog to Llanbedr an elderly Whitley bomber, to be used to tow target drogues for gunners? It was one of those incomprehensible wartime apportionments of duties that made no sense to the individuals so deployed. Perhaps they thought they were usefully resting him. Perhaps the newly-established No 9 Bombing and Gunnery School at Penrhos actually needed all the help it could get. Either way it was like giving an engraver finger-paints: he'd be bound to get frustrated and careless.

On recent evenings the peninsula lay in red light peaceably, like the forearm of an animal curled in slumber. It was cloudy on this night, however, with variegated masses of cloud moving contrarily as the wind, confused by the irregular heights of the Welsh coast scattered in all directions.

When the mountain came at him out of the mist he had, in fact, been singing:

> 'Hey, tell me, doesn't that look like Dixieland?
> Sure, that looks like Dixieland.
> Doesn't that look like Alabam'?
> Why, sure that's Birmingham.
> Is there any place so nice?
> Do I have to ask you twice?
> Yes, sir! Yes, sir! That's my paradise!'

And there, suddenly, was this glistening outcrop of granite, a ridiculous jutting, like a feature of physiognomy. And such is the power of song that the melody continued to echo with distant mockery in his brain:

> 'Mr Lindbergh made Paree,
> But I made God's own heaven, you see,
> And there ain't no land like Dixieland to me.'

Had he not made an equally heroic journey? The question insisted itself in this last quarter-minute as a kind of justification. Not this journey itself, of course, but the journey which his training and the conduct of the war had required from him, the journey which was the tale of his adventures and of his anonymity.

For he had become a man without a significant history. Nothing of his past seemed recoverable. It had simply

19

been knocked away like the wooden supports at the launching of a vessel. He was simply like all the others now, an exhausted fanatic, a reader of the instruments, a collector of targets and trophies. The inheritor of Lindbergh, perhaps, but no more.

The fissured wall of mountain, with its few spread ledges of heather and its damp surface that meant a dripping cave somewhere below, or perhaps a stream, was an irrelevance. Its sudden total presence through the glass before him as the mist lifted seemed like an animate calculation of surprise, and therefore a kind of impersonation. It was an outrage: a mountain with apparent motives of its own.

He pulled the stick as hard as he could, as though shutting a stiff door on the demon of his dreams, trapping it, but being able neither to shut it out, nor safely to release it, the only solution the impossible one of squeezing it to oblivion. But he sensed it was too late.

He thought of all the previous and recent dangers that he had survived despite the apparently greater odds of human intention and enmity. The worst, last August, had involved bailing out over the Channel.

He had been one of six aircraft patrolling the south coast. Towards the end of their patrol they had sighted about nine Messerschmidt 109s, and had engaged. He remembered how that first sick recognition of the inevitable, that drained sensation of fear and anticipation, had made him belch, and even as the nearest of the Messerschmidts had started clambering away from him and he had pursued, he had tasted again the Marmite sandwich he had eaten hours before. He had opened up at a hundred yards and the Messerschmidt had caught fire at the third burst.

He had turned right and attacked another Messerschmidt, firing a burst from astern. Its port wing folded up.

20

As he levelled out, a Junkers 88 flew across his path. He did a quarter attack. The Junkers' starboard engine emitted black smoke and it half-rolled into the sea.

He was then hit underneath by a cannon shell. As he did a complete turn to the right, he saw a Messerschmidt 110 flying past, as though quite unconcerned, a toy. He did a beam attack on it. The Messerschmidt's starboard engine smoked and it turned on its back and fell into the sea.

When he looked in the other direction there was a large number of enemy aircraft, and his Hurricane was hit a number of times. Two shells smashed the instrument panel and three more struck underneath.

The engine stopped and flames appeared over the wing roots. He was at 400 feet and tried to get out, but couldn't, so pulled the stick back from a crouching position on the seat. He had never felt so calm.

As the Hurricane stalled, he got over the port side and took a header off the plane. He was being fired at, so he delayed pulling the ripcord as long as possible above the sea.

He had left the fighter at 800 feet. The parachute worked perfectly, and he descended like a puff of August thistle, the high blue all above him chalked with smoke.

He was picked up by a paddle steamer, and landed at Margate.

This, and days like it, when outlandish peril had almost been systematised into a jaunt or routine, now seemed diminished in memory. The names of the dead, Crawford, Silver, Driven, Stike, Blondworm, Rogers, Jauncey, Price, Leverbarrow, Headlong, Lacey, Beskett, were now merely a legendary recital, half magic, half play, like the familiar terms of a game whose actual rules had been forgotten. They had swung into the sky and then tumbled from it, 21 and no one could think why. It had something to do with a miraculously averted threat of invasion, a defence of the island citadel. Everyone knew that. But why it had to happen was mysterious. The behaviour of the aircraft, disobedient to physical laws, was an incalculable performance of energy and initiative. Harvesters looked up from the Downs, shading their eyes. That secret was as far beyond them as the hatching and vagrant flight of butterflies. It was noisy, outrageous, colourful, hideous. It was the secret of youth.

And now here was a mountain, the oldest thing in sight except the sky. For millions of years it had had nothing to do at all. It shouldered its little epaulettes of heather, grudgingly, careless of the wild goats that stalked its lower reaches like patriarchs in exile. Its cracked granite face leaked in the eroding wind. It wore the pretence of suffering that mere existence could always contrive. It was a sham. It was heartless.

It was like a hand put up by the oldest of the Fates, tired at last of relenting, ready for her final pronouncement: 'Thus far, but no further! This was always waiting for you!'

The nose of the aircraft strained upwards. The mountain face came nearer. It was like looking through the window of an ascending lift. He was close enough to see saplings of ash protruding from crevices.

Knowing that there was nothing to be done, knowing that there was no time to do any more, knowing that there was no time even for knowing, he could only feel a strange kind of exhilaration.

> 'And doesn't that smell like ham and eggs?
> No, that smells like bacon and eggs.
> Bacon and eggs? Ham and eggs?
> Oh gee!'

Something came off the undercarriage. Even as everything happened, he felt that it might somehow be controlled. Had he almost avoided the cliff?

Annie Lloyd in the fields below with her sheep could see that he had not. As the plane had emerged from the cloud she could not believe that it was so big, even though it was making such a great noise. A piece of it bounced down the mountain like dislodged scree. The cloud obscured it again, but not before she had seen it fatally tilted. She did not know whether to run towards it or away from it. The cloud moved on. It was swirling steadily over the *bwlch* like a liquid being slowly poured, but thinning intermittently as though being poured with a not quite steady hand. The plane seemed to be ploughing through the heather at the top of the cliff, one wing folding over above it. There was a burst of flame which immediately lifted and seemed to go out, like, as Annie said later to Largo Evans, 'a spark up a chimney'.

Men rushed up from the villages, not knowing what they could do, but knowing that they had to put down what they were doing and climb the single-track road and the quarry paths to the scene of the crash. There were pieces of the undercarriage and wing strewn up the slopes at the foot of the cliff, just by the big Hendre Fawr stone. The pieces were warm. It took them twice as long to climb the last few hundred feet. Some of them were used to moving injured men over difficult ground after quarry accidents, and had come prepared. But as they stumbled towards the smoking wreckage through the scorched and flattened heather they had no hopes of finding the pilot in a rescuable condition.

They could see that he had virtually missed the cliff and had effected some sort of crash-landing on the part of the mountain that started to flatten out before it rose again to 23

the crown. There had been a fire, as Annie said, but it had
for some reason quickly burned out.

What was he doing there? What a terrible mistake it
was. They spent the whole night on the mountain, not
out of morbid curiosity (though there were a few private
mementoes taken away from the wreckage) but because
they needed instructions from the ambulance that was
called out from Caernarvon up the lonely mountain road,
and which could go no further than the bend of the
road by the stream at Gallt-y-ceiliog. They had to use the
greatest care in bringing the damaged pilot down, because
they found that he was, in fact, still breathing.

3

One Tuesday afternoon when classes were over, David was married to Jill Simpson. The wedding took place in a corner of the playground that nobody could see from the school building itself. It was a blind spot suitable for initiations and persecutions.

The ceremony was conducted by Toffee Mynors and George Robinson, and it took the form of a trial. David knew that he was guilty of being hated by Toffee Mynors, but he did not know why Jill Simpson was on trial. They had to kiss the stumps of Robbo's fingers, but Jill refused. David knew that he should have refused, too. He wanted to push Toffee Mynors over and run away. He wanted to hit him. He even wanted to hit Robbo, though he thought Robbo was his friend. When Jill refused, Toffee Mynors didn't know what to do. He tried to make David put his hand up Jill's skirt, but David said that he wouldn't do that. When Miss Mackie was seen coming towards them, the wedding broke up hurriedly. The priests ran into the lavatories, leaving their victims to invent explanations for Miss Mackie.

'Are you still hanging around here?' she said, clapping her hands slightly, as though they were chickens and not a bridal pair. 'Be off home with you now.'

Miss Mackie always reminded David of thin burnt toast. Her fingers were cold when she showed him how to sew raffia, and she had a line of dark hair on her upper lip and between her eyebrows, so that sometimes it seemed as if she only had one long eyebrow.

'Was David behaving himself, dear?' she asked Jill. 'Why did Sidney and George run off?'

Jill looked down at the ground, and David looked at the buttons of Miss Mackie's cardigan. They were horny, with ridges in them.

'It's too late for you all to be here still,' she continued. 'You must go home directly to your tea.'

'Yes, Miss Mackie,' they replied.

'Isn't your father collecting you, Jill?' she asked.

'He's at Seaton Hall this week, miss.'

'Shall you take the bus, then?'

'Yes, miss.'

David walked with her to the bus stop. Or rather, Jill walked to the bus stop and David walked beside her, running sometimes to keep up with her. When he had to stop to tie his shoelace, she did not wait for him.

She stood as still as the bus stop, waiting for a Number 4. Her face was pale, and she did not look at him.

'It wasn't my fault,' said David.

He looked at the thick blonde plait that hung stiffly down her back. Close to, you could hear the little rustling noise that it made against the collar of her dress. It was held together at the end with an orange rubber band.

'I thought you were my friend,' said Jill.

He had never touched her plait, though he had seen others do it. Smaller girls especially might run up behind her, lift it and let it fall back like a door-knocker, or give it a little tug like a bell, and then run away giggling. Jill might very well not do anything more than give her head

26

a slight shake as though annoyed by a fly. She always kept her head very straight.

'I am,' said David. 'I am. That's why they did it.'

Then suddenly she turned and smiled at him, and the bus sailed up like a chariot of the gods. David himself climbed on board in a trance, and bought both the tickets.

'Two halfpenny ones, please.'

With the change from the threepenny bit he made two copper monocles for his eyes, and Jill laughed, catching the pennies when they fell and screwing them back between his brow and cheek. He could feel her breath on his face as she did this, but he could see nothing.

He didn't care that he was on a bus going in the wrong direction. He could have travelled for ever. But when he felt the bus going past the roundabout and saw that they were passing Stillman's, and George and Taylor's, he felt that he had to get off. When he looked up, she was waving from the bus window.

'Come to tea tomorrow,' she shouted.

He nodded, and waved back.

When he got home, Granny was in the kitchen with Mr Elswick, who was helping her to unblock the wastepipe. He was crouched under the sink with a spanner.

'Can I go to tea with Jill Simpson tomorrow?' asked David.

'Miss Simpson, the doctor's daughter,' said Mr Elswick loudly from beneath the sink. Then he coughed. David wondered if he coughed so much to remind everyone that he was too ill to be in the army.

'Did they ask you then, David?' said Granny.

'Well, Jill asked me,' he replied.

'You'd better behave yourself,' said Mr Elswick, unnecessarily.

27

'David always behaves nicely,' said Granny. 'Don't you, David?'

'Don't spit in the jam,' said Mr Elswick. He laughed and coughed at the same time. He was now working a black rubber hand-pump up and down in the sink.

'Go outside, will you, David?' he asked. 'Tell us if anything's happening.'

David went outside into the back yard and looked at the drain.

'What's supposed to be happening?' he shouted.

'Is there any water coming out?'

'No.'

Later, Granny made Mr Elswick a cup of tea, and he told them about Dr Simpson's work at the Rehabilitation Unit at Seaton Hall.

'All those poor boys,' said Granny. 'It's a grand job of work.'

'It is, that,' said Mr Elswick, dipping a biscuit in his tea. 'And he keeps the practice going as well. He must be up all hours.'

David watched the soggy end of the biscuit curl dangerously as Mr Elswick lifted it to his lips. When he had eaten the biscuit, Granny pushed the barrel towards him and made him take another. She was always attentive to Mr Elswick, although she said the Elswicks kept a dirty house. When Mrs Elswick came round to take Granny to the whist drive, she was often kept waiting in the hall, and Granny contradicted things she said. Mrs Elswick never seemed to notice. She never seemed to have anything to do, but was quite happy to sit in Granny's front room and listen to whoever was talking. Mr Elswick drove a taxi, and quite often he didn't have much to do either, but would sit outside his house and nod to the neighbours as they passed. He took another biscuit.

'I reckon you'll not have trouble with the drain now,' he said. His teeth made a slight clacking sound as he spoke, and David could see soggy biscuit between them like the pointing in old brickwork.

'Can I go then?' asked David.

'Of course you can go,' said Granny.

'I mean to Jill Simpson's,' went on David. 'You didn't say.'

'Of course I said, didn't I,' said Granny. 'Don't be late.' She sounded dismissive.

'It's not today,' said David. 'It's tomorrow.'

'I know that,' said Granny. 'No need to make a song and dance about it.'

'A song and a dance,' said Mr Elswick. 'A smile and a farewell.'

The next day David went with Jill all the way on the top of the bus to her house. Between the bottom of her pleated grey skirt and the folded tops of her white stockings her pink knees lay together perfectly matched like a pair of cards at Pelmanism. They were chubby, dimpled and unscarred, and surrounded by tiny golden hairs. The bus began to sway down leafy lanes, and branches occasionally whipped the windows. David flinched at the sudden noise and the strange scrabbling of green at the glass, but Jill sat perfectly still with her hands on her lap, looking out.

The Simpsons had a big house that you could walk all round, and laurel bushes that you could hide in. Jill's mother brought cake and lemonade to the bottom of the garden where Jill had put up the wigwam under an apple tree. David knocked his lemonade over, but Jill didn't offer to share hers. She drank it slowly, looking at him over the glass. When they ate their cakes, she ate all the icing off first, easing it up with her tongue and nibbling at it with her teeth. That was all they had. They didn't have a proper tea.

29

Unlike his attic, Jill's room was a proper bedroom with a carpet and its own furniture. He was amazed at some of the things she had, like a white mouse in a cage and a collection of miniature china goblets, urns and coal-scuttles all with brightly coloured heraldic shields on them. She also had a green papier mâché top hat which she put on every time she entered the room. It sat on her ears with fine wisps of fair hair curling from beneath it, and made her plait even harder to resist pulling.

Her brother Robin showed them his air pistol, but he wouldn't let them fire it. While he was working the mechanism David watched his pale round face, and the pink tongue resting on the bottom lip in concentration. His fair hair lay over his forehead, loose and dry. David wondered why he didn't brush it back with brilliantine. When the pistol was loaded, Robin fired at apples in the apple tree, but didn't hit any. He laughed, and went away.

It was quite late when Dr Simpson came back from Seaton Hall. David heard Jill's mother telling him that he should drive him home. Dr Simpson groaned, and they talked in quieter voices. There was a pan boiling on the stove, and the smell of food.

David was hot with running in the garden, and had come inside to use the toilet. The toilet paper was of a kind that he had never seen before, on a roll, and there were photographs of men in cricketing flannels. When he came out, Dr Simpson smiled at him and said he was going to take him home. David wondered why he wasn't going to be given any tea, but remembered to be polite and say thank you. The car had a leathery smell like Mr Elswick's taxi, but he was allowed to sit at the front and he noticed curious faces at several windows when they drew up at Viewforth Road.

30   'Well,' said Granny. 'Did you enjoy yourself?'

David wondered if he had enjoyed himself. He was hungry, but he didn't want to say that he had not had his tea.

'Yes,' he said. 'It was grand.'

'The drain's blocked again,' said Granny.

'Shall I have a go?' he offered.

'It won't do much good.'

David worked the rubber pump carefully in the sink, standing on a chair so that he could be right on top of it. Jacko came into the kitchen and said scornfully:

'You'll never do that. Here.'

He took the handle from David and moved it quickly up and down, splashing water everywhere. It didn't work, and he soon lost interest. David watched him as he slouched about the kitchen, putting his finger in the jam and licking it, emptying the contents of a box of matches and cramming them back in anyhow. David supposed that he was older than Robin Simpson, but he did not behave as though he was. He was waiting for Fred to call for him. They were going to the Imperial to see the musical.

'Are you going to take me with you?' asked Granny.

'Get away,' said Jacko. 'You've seen it anyway.'

'I never have,' said Granny.

'You have, you know,' said Jacko decisively. He sat down at the kitchen table.

'Never,' said Granny.

'I thought you went on Tuesday,' replied Jacko uncertainly.

'No,' said Granny triumphantly.

'I haven't seen it either,' put in David.

Jacko turned on him.

'Well, I'm not taking you for a start, you toffee-nosed little bastard.'

Before Granny's hand could reach his head, he was up and out of his chair, skipping across the kitchen.

31

The doorbell rang.

'There, that's Fred now,' said Jacko, escaping.

When he had gone, Granny went back to the sink, bending underneath it to look at the wastepipe. David wondered if she would notice if he sneaked past her to the larder. There might be something there that wouldn't be missed: a few spoonfuls of cold rice pudding, perhaps, or some dried fruit. He was so hungry that he might even have tried to steal one of the eggs preserved in the large brown crock under the bottom shelf, though he wouldn't have known how to cook it. He had once tried to lift one away from the acrid-smelling adhesive mass and cracked it. He would have been content with raiding the biscuit barrel, which had been taken back to its proper place on the sideboard in the front room.

He wondered what it would be like to have a mother like Mrs Simpson. He could not imagine her wearing a house-coat or bending under a sink. She moved slowly, like the Queen in newsreels, as cool as the ice clinking in a glass of lemonade.

He wondered what it would be like to have an older brother or an uncle like Robin Simpson, who wore a little boy's short-sleeved aertex shirts and didn't mind showing him how things worked. He wondered what it would be like to have Jill Simpson for a sister. She would not be like any other sister that he knew, like Robbo's fat little sister Ann who giggled, or Ritchie Dale's sister Gloria who went out with a different boy each week. She would be his own age, like his twin. She would be quiet and understanding and loyal and would never wear lipstick. They would grow older together and put their arms round each other's shoulders. After all, they had been married by Toffee Mynors. It had been meant to be a spiteful joke, but David knew that it was really the unthinking acknowledgment of a truth.

4

Time had abandoned him. He was only aware that it was like going into a tunnel. Having gone into a tunnel, he had, simply by continuing, to come out of it. But there was nothing to tell him how long he had been there or where he had come from, just as the way through a tunnel abandons all landscape or geography. The darkness surrounding him was like a puzzle, and his being aware at all was the very first clue to it. He had no idea how to handle this clue. He sensed that only the solution to the puzzle could tell him how.

But now, at least, he knew that there was something to be endured. What had begun was continuing. What continued might change. All he had to do was to stick it out. Knowing this brought with it the shadow of a memory of some previous state of being. He seemed to be on the brink of remembering what it was, as close to it almost as a swimmer short of breath is when about to break up through the surface of the water. But the revelation was again withheld from him. That bright surface on the other side of darkness was something that a door in his own mind kept out. His ignorance was some kind of struggle with himself, a voluntary silencing.

He sank back again.

What a relief to turn from certain kinds of knowledge! Some small suspicion, the merest lost child of an idea adrift in his head like a wraith, was enough for him to slam the cruel doors of forgetting. What was this suspicion? No, no. Better not to know, better not to follow it in the dark mazes. Shut it out. Shut it out.

The pictures in his head resumed their extraordinary colour and animation. He was casually present at aerobatic ceremonies in the deeply recessed ceiling of a Tudor library. Its ancient rafters were so chamfered, carved and polished that they looked more like totems than roof-structure. The mood was one of excited witness, part pride, part tourist admiration. The sense of wonder was doubly thrilling, as being both given and received. Proud to be there, he knew that something was to be required of him.

The boys buckled on thick-soled white shoes that were as formal as equipment for fencing. Devotion to books was abandoned, as at the sudden announcement of holiday; and yet there was at the same time something routine about the changed purpose of the vast chamber, in which the heavy volumes were not so much casually abandoned as left in studied positions, as if part of the ceremony, like markers in a game. Any audience that there may have been was invisible. The spectacle was enough in itself. And yet there was an energising sense of performance.

Even as one of the boys leaped at the wooden panelling with one foot extended, springing not only back from it as in nature he must, but upwards as well, all sense of hostly deference, even of apology for such quaint customs, of dismissal, of the possibility of moving on from here to other chambers where a conversation or purpose might be resumed, all this was put aside. The absolute necessity now was spectacle, encouragement, ritual, even participation. The first boy had grasped a beam, had reversed his body, and used the momentum to swing even higher, though backwards, into the ceiling. As others propelled themselves into motion, traversing desks, gaps between desks, and whole aisles and naves of the library, there was a sense of swarming, like the manning of a ship. And yet the spirit of the display did not cease to be ceremonious, even solemn. Their movements were precise, as if tradition had decreed the absolute physical constraints of certain heights or distances. On the other hand the learned disorder of the chamber presented a variety of unforeseen hazards, requiring changes of course, split-second swapping of places, extemporising of jumps. An apparent object of the exercise was to traverse the room without touching the floor. But this had, in time, become so easy that it was a mere ground-bass to the theme of ascent. To remind the observer of the function of the chamber, there was incense and dazzling music in a finely-judged excess, allowing the observing mind to swing between the idea of ship, gymnasium, library and church, much as the boys swung higher and higher from embrasure to embrasure, as if seeking an unlikely but hidden source of light within the limitless roof.

Oh, what joy! If he could stay here for ever, he could ignore that other world lying beyond the light. But this new knowledge of passing time, with its unwelcome consciousness of the direction of the tunnel, was a sign that he could not do so. The tunnel was like a tube propelling him forward, like that other force, the reverse of gravity, which restored the buoyant diver to the broken skin of the deep pool. And the marvellous extemporisations of climbing, the trapeze-like exchanges in the heavy rafters, were also an intended image of his future.

35

He was no longer watching. The fond, proprietorial or custodial mood was broken. He himself had reached the shelves beyond the upper shelves, straddling the little wicket gates and black-timbered catwalks that served the dusty galleries of the rarer books. Cornices were stepping-stones. He knew all eyes were on him now. He was the hero. He was ascending further than the others. He could hear, far below, the massed gasps of wonder as he tight-roped a beam through shafts of light from the now-visible and almost attainable scant turrets let into the roof. Through one of these shoulder-width apertures, lined with white clapboard, he knew he had finally to push. In the last stages there could be no footing, only the achieved momentum towards the cheered revelation of the half-open fanlights. And there he was! The music intensified. The light thundered. And the ambience of exploit that was momentarily his was concentrated even more sharply into his own daring selfhood, at first constrained by the turret, with its cap of glass like the inside of a miniature light-house, and then constrained only by its returning identity. It was a remembered thing, the body he had not lost.

Somewhere a tiny atom of reasoning pleaded, as a naked creature might plead with the forced circumstances of its birth. The reasoning made no sense. It argued for the recognition of a miracle. It argued for tenacity, gratitude, the need to establish the difference between dream and reality, between lost consciousness and the consciousness of lost consciousness. He felt as detached from this idiot reasoning as he felt detached from his monster body. Both were telling him that he was still alive, one by weighing fine distinctions, the other by roaring out one simple truth. This truth was a vile horror that had been insistently present even in his oblivion: pain.

36   It was a totality, an irreversible error. It was beyond

anything that belonged to him. He belonged to it. It was an otherness. Like light, you could not switch it off without abandoning the world defined by it. Drifting awake, he was caught in the eddy and flow of it. He could no more contemplate it from outside in order to measure or assess it than he could move upstream, or squeeze back into his tunnel. It was, and he was it.

5

It soon became clear that Jacko was likely to be called up.

David was under the table in the front room one evening, keeping Belgian bridges open for his fleet of Dinky toys, when he heard Jean and his Granny talking about it.

'I don't want him to go, Jean.'

'He'll have to go, mother. He's nearly nineteen.'

There was an indistinct sound, as though Granny had started to say something else, and the clink of a teacup. In his green room with its screwed eaves of table David felt safe from the conversation. He was not expected to have views on these important questions, but he knew that if he had, for example, been sitting at the table painting, the very guardedness of the grown-ups in talking in front of him would have been a constraint upon him, a kind of involvement.

'Don't, mother.'

There was a stifled sigh, and after a moment Granny left the room with the tray.

There were other witnesses in the front room: the cut-glass bowl of fruit on the sideboard and the glass of the biscuit barrel hiding behind the silver panels of its container. The glass-fronted cupboard on the left of the fireplace was another averted lens, its trophies and ornaments inside like a head full of memories that distracted from the present: the glass lighthouse of coloured stripes of sand from the Isle of Wight; the china doll with the movable straw hat that revealed a second face, Chinese, at the back of its head; the photograph of Grandpa at the top of the front steps holding a black spaniel. David knew that the spaniel's name was Bob, but he could remember him no more clearly than Grandpa.

Captain Heart leaped from his '36 Buick, both thumbs in the belt-loops of his trousers, his legs straddled, his broad-brimmed hat pushed slightly back from his sunburned face.

'We need reinforcements,' he announced. 'I intend to raise the age of conscription for military service to fifty one. I also intend to lower it to eighteen and a half. Unmarried women between the ages of twenty and thirty will also be liable. Can anyone drive an ambulance?'

Two crouching Sioux were immediately drafted, and a grey turkey with viridian and crimson trimmings. The convoy was now able to proceed, and Captain Heart climbed back into the Buick.

Casualties were heavy. The daily figures were written on a notepad, and sorrowful speeches were made. The bridges were kept open, but at great cost. Captain Heart was asked to appear at Buckingham Palace, where the King gave him a medal.

'Thank you, your Majesty,' he said in reply. 'But I couldn't have done a thing without Des Mullard and Jacko Turner. They worked round the clock, and kept the Indians in order.'

Des was David's father, who was going to come and see him when he next had leave. He was working on the Lancaster bombers that were going to blast Hitler to kingdom come.

39

Jacko had as little love for Hitler as anyone else, but didn't see why his momentous life should be interrupted to defeat a dictator.

'That Mrs Thesiger,' he said one day with a sniff. 'Asked me why I wasn't in uniform.'

'What did you say, Jacko?' asked his sister.

'What do you think I said?'

'How do I know what you said?'

'I didn't say anything, did I?'

Jacko was slouching in the kitchen, running his finger round the batter bowl.

'What could I say?' he muttered. 'The old bitch. The war doesn't mean a thing to her, it doesn't. She gets all the chickens and eggs she wants out at Langley's.'

'You don't go short yourself.'

'Well, I mind my own business.'

'I expect she was concerned,' said Jean. 'Ritchie Dale's been drafted.'

'Concerned? Concerned about Ritchie?' Jacko laughed bitterly. 'She's always complaining about Ritchie's bike. She's glad to see the back of him.'

'Not the only one in this street, I can tell you,' said Jean.

'You're all the same, you are,' retorted Jacko. 'You were all over Ritchie Dale not long ago.'

'Me?' Jean was outraged. 'Never!'

'Yes, well,' Jacko muttered. 'That Mrs Thesiger. You've seen her with mother, all nodding and clucking. Remember when I did that paper round? Remember?'

'Yes,' said Jean. 'It didn't last long, did it?'

'I did that bloody paper round, didn't I? Never mind how long I did it. Just ask me who didn't give me a tip at Christmas. Just ask me who out of the whole street didn't give me a tip at Christmas.'

'You've been on about this before.'

'I'm not surprised. Bit of a scandal, wasn't it? You're not telling me that Mrs Thesiger is short of the ready?'

'I don't expect so.'

On Sundays they all went out to the cemetery to put flowers on Grandpa's grave. Whatever the weather, Granny would button up her best coat, standing upright in front of the mirror in the hall. Then she would put on her hat. She was on parade.

At the cemetery, Jacko and Jean went on ahead, taking side paths round the lawns, cutting corners. Granny gripped David's hand tightly in hers and kept to the main paths. In that way they approached the grave at different speeds and from different directions. It was like a board game, with counters.

At the grave there was nothing to do but stand and watch while Granny changed the flowers. There ought to have been something to do. Jacko stood with his hands by his side as though listening to a trumpet casting stillness over the whole suburbs of the deceased. Jean gave her mother her arm to help her get up. David didn't like to see Granny kneeling awkwardly. She wasn't made to bend.

More than once Granny said to David: 'I wish your mother was here.' He imagined her by his side, holding his other hand, or walking with her brother and sister ahead of them, three children together among the clasped hands and obelisks of granite remembrance.

It was not till later that David realised that Granny meant that she wished that his mother's grave was there, so that she could put flowers on it.

Then they came home for their dinner, and if there was anything wrong with the Yorkshire pudding it was probably because Jacko had been dipping his fingers in it.

During the weekdays the house was quiet when David came back from school. Granny might be peeling potatoes.

41

Sometimes she might be upstairs having a rest. Jacko and Jean didn't get in till later because they both went out to work. Jacko worked at Brickfields. He had a good job, in the drawing office. Jean was an assistant at Stillman's. She sometimes brought little trophies home in her handbag, pencils and rubber-bands and things, or the end of a roll of paper from the till. Once she brought David some thick wax crayons. She said they were chucking them out because the purple one was broken, but she told David not to show them to Granny.

Jacko would be incredulous.

'Did you pinch them things?' he would ask, loudly.

'Be quiet, will you,' said Jean, shushing him.

'You're a bloody klepto, you are. They'll be putting you away.'

'Leave off, Jacko.'

'Don't ask me to come and visit you,' he replied. 'I'm not coming with a file in a cake.'

Jean would shrug, and go to her room. She didn't go out much in the evenings now. Sid Molyneux had taken her dancing at the Savoy, and Jean had had arguments with Granny, who said he was flash. He hadn't asked her out again, anyway. Phyllis had been sent to work at the rehabilitation unit at Seaton Hall. They made her sleep in the nurses' quarters because she was on duty at all hours, and only got home at weekends.

Jacko was convinced that his job at Brickfields meant that he wouldn't be called up. He said it was protected.

Mr Elswick thought otherwise.

'Protected? Is it heck as like.'

'It's in the national interest, Mr Elswick.'

'It's in the national interest to fight this war, lad. And to win it.'

42   'It wouldn't be much good if everyone joined up and

got killed,' said Jacko. 'What would we be fighting for then?'

'We're fighting for what's what,' said Mr Elswick. 'We're fighting for civilisation.'

Jacko didn't say anything. He had started to go out with Sylvia Elswick, and didn't want to argue with her father. Mr Elswick liked to lay down the law, Jacko said. According to Jacko, you might think Mr Elswick talked a lot, but you had to listen to him in his own house to get the full force of it. He never did anything. He just told everyone else what to do. It was no wonder that their house was always in a mess. And Mrs Elswick never talked back. She couldn't even ask him to get the coal in. She asked Sylvia.

Sylvia Elswick was a small dark girl with heavily-lidded eyes that always seemed to be half-closed. Her nose was always half-blocked, too. She never closed her mouth, and her upper lip was pinched upwards towards her nostrils as if for the convenient passage of air.

When Jacko first announced that he was going to the Imperial with Sylvia Elswick, Jean was incredulous.

'And what does Fred think about that?' she asked.

'It's got nothing to do with Fred.'

'If I remember rightly, you and Fred used to chase her down the back with daggers.'

'Not real daggers,' he said.

'That's not the point.' Jean stopped what she was doing and laughed. 'The point was, Jacko, that you and Fred persecuted Sylvia Elswick. You treated her like muck.'

'We was just kids then, Jean. Don't be daft.'

'You're the daft one, Jacko,' said Jean, turning back to the sink. 'She's still just a kid, isn't she? She's got adenoids, too.'

Jean shuddered, and went on:

'I don't know what you see in her, I really don't.'

Jacko smiled mysteriously.

43

'Well, you're a girl. You're not meant to, are you?'

Captain Heart called a meeting of the entire Division that afternoon. His mouth was pale and drawn. The room fell silent as soon as he came in.

'Comrades,' he began, his eyes sweeping the attentive mass of faces. 'I have realised for some time that morale is not at the moment at its highest. I may be forced to put even younger unmarried women into full-time work in the fighting services. I shall begin to interview the conscripts immediately.'

The first conscript was Sylvia Elswick. She stood before Captain Heart sullenly in her green hat and worn yellow smock, a bucket tightly gripped in each hand.

'You may put the buckets down if you wish,' said the Captain in a kindly voice.

She did not respond.

'I am only trying to make things easy for you,' he went on. 'For you and for Private Jacko Turner. I understand that you wish to fight side by side. The War Office is prepared to allow this because we need all the manpower – and womanpower – we can get. It will not be long before a Second Front is opened against the Nazi terror. How are your adenoids?'

It appeared that her adenoids were so bad that they prevented her from speaking at all, so the rest of the morning was devoted to a lengthy operation to remove them. Captain Heart carried her round the ward, and the other patients smiled at her, and said wasn't she a brave girl? After the operation she was given bacon to eat, because it was good for her, though her head felt funny and she could taste blood in her mouth.

After that, she was sent to the front.

David wondered what would happen when everyone had gone off to fight the war. Wasn't Jacko right in what he had said to Mr Elswick? If everyone was fighting, there'd be no one to fight for. Mr Elswick said we were fighting for civilisation, and that must mean the same as civilians. But soon there wouldn't be many civilians left. Ritchie Dale had joined up. He turned up one weekend on leave with his hair clipped close all above his ears and right up to the crown of his head. He came round to see Jacko, and Jean burst out laughing.

'I'm sorry, Ritchie, I really am. But it makes you look about ten years old.'

'I don't think I'm talking to you, Jean Turner,' said Ritchie. 'Unless you want to buy my bike.'

Nobody, not even Jacko, wanted to buy Ritchie's motor-bike. For one thing, he wanted at least £30 for it.

'Get away,' said Jacko. 'Go and sell it to Lord Beaver-brook. If I had that sort of money I'd buy a saxophone, wouldn't I?'

'Yeah,' said Ritchie. 'I reckon you would.'

'And what would I do for petrol, eh?'

Ritchie smirked.

'You're in pretty thick with old Elswick, aren't you? No shortage of petrol there.'

'Never,' said Jacko. 'Nothing doing.'

'You can't get very far on a saxophone, can you?' said Ritchie.

'I'm not getting a bloody saxophone, am I?' said Jacko in exasperation. 'That's the whole point. I'm skint.'

They saw Ritchie to the gate. Jean was washing dishes, but she came out of the front door drying a plate with a tea towel, just so that she could see the back of Ritchie's head as he lumbered down the steps. She leaned against the front door with her knees sagging, creased with laughter.

'I was a fugitive from a chain gang,' she called out. Ritchie turned and glared.

45

'It'll be your turn soon, don't you worry,' he snarled. 'You know what they do to you in the ATS. Shave you everywhere.'

'Ritchie Dale!' exclaimed Jean in outrage.

Jacko aimed a cuff at the offending head, but Ritchie swaggered into the road. He turned back with a grin.

'Lice,' he called out.

'Get away, go on,' Jacko shouted back.

David, who had followed Jean to the front door, shouted: 'Good riddance to bad rubbish!'

'Ssh,' said Jean. 'You keep out of it, David.'

Ritchie raised two fingers at them all and disappeared down the street.

Later, when Granny heard about it, she asked Jacko why he hadn't bargained for the motor bike.

'I thought you were keen on having one,' she said. 'He might take a lot less for it, seeing as how he's got to get rid of it, and you've got all that saved up.'

Jacko grimaced.

'Yes, well,' he said. 'I might not be around much longer to get the use of it, might I?'

It was the first time that he had acknowledged the imminence of his call-up. From that time on he became thoughtful and silent. He went out far less, and if Sylvia came to tea he hardly spoke to her. He didn't speak much to anyone.

It was left to Granny and to Jean to be agreeable to Sylvia. Jean would ask her about her former boy-friend, or if she was planning to get a job.

'Oh no,' said Sylvia. 'It's not hardly worth it now.'

Jean confronted Jacko with that remark later, when Sylvia had gone.

'What was that meant to mean?' she asked accusingly.

46   'How do I know?' replied Jacko.

Jean sniffed.

'It meant something. I know that.'

David quite liked Sylvia Elswick. She always took notice of him, and offered him sweets. Not everyone took notice of him, not for his own sake, anyway. If anyone said anything it was usually something about his poor mother, or to ask if he'd heard from his father. He wished that people would take him at face value, as Sylvia did.

'Have a liquorice allsort, David,' Sylvia would say, holding out a crumpled bag.

'Thank you.'

'Ooh, wait a minute,' she would say. 'Did you take a coconut one? How many coconut ones are there left?'

David was quite willing to put it back.

'No, go on. It's all right.'

And she would look carefully into the bag to see how many of each kind were left.

David wondered what her attraction was for Jacko. She was, compared with Jean or Phyllis, distinctly flat-chested. Perhaps bosoms simply grew larger as you grew older, like Granny or Mrs Thesiger, who were immense. But their bosoms, large as they were, somehow didn't have anything of the available attraction of Jean's or Phyllis's. they seemed merely private and corporeal, and not for use: rich in resource, yes, in history, in implication, but theoretical only. It was like the difference between a bag of liquorice allsorts that someone was offering you, and a whole jar of them on the shelf of the sweetshop. David reflected that the attraction of the bag was, after all, whether it was being offered or not. Sylvia Elswick always offered hers, even when it turned out (as was sometimes the case) that there were none left, or only a couple of the thin black cylinders, stuck together.

That made them seem all the more exciting.

6

Everyone knew it was the day when they were going to do all they could for the new boy. There was an air of purpose in the corridors, and Sister was quite short with old Ted when he wheeled round the trolley with the clean sheets. Instead of passing the time of day with him, perhaps over a cup of tea, she reminded him that he was late. Ted shrugged.

He told Mrs Castle about it, speaking to her broad back as she scrubbed out the boilers.

'They've got a hard case today,' he said, lighting up a cigarette. 'That lad they brought in from Bangor.'

'Aye,' breathed Mrs Castle as she worked.

'Charlie Barnes says no one's allowed near him, but it's worse than anything we had in 1940.'

'Poor boy,' said Mrs Castle.

Charlie Barnes had been one of the porters who had brought him in from the ambulance, and he could tell it was very bad, everything bandaged and more tubes than he had ever seen. They kept the curtains drawn round him in the ward, and a nurse had to sit in there all the time. Sister had said it was a miracle.

They called him the new boy because nobody knew his

name yet. Bangor had telephoned to say that the name they had put down wasn't the right one, and there was some difficulty with the Air Ministry. The Registrar said he was sorry, but there was nothing they could do just yet. Sister had said that wasn't good enough.

'You had him for weeks,' she said. 'What am I expected to do about it from up here?'

'We'll let you know as soon as we hear,' was the reply.

Poor lad, thought Sister. Didn't he have a mother and father? Wouldn't they want to know where he was? Perhaps he had a sweetheart. That was a different matter. She had seen young girls come, and step down frowning from the bus, wearing all their best clothes as if they were going to church. Well, it was an ordeal. You couldn't pretend otherwise. Some of them could cope. Especially if it was just hands. Men could look so helpless in bandaged hands, like great babies in mittens. But faces were different. There's everything in a face, and when the face goes there doesn't seem anything to cling to. Many of the girls couldn't cope. All of them were frightened.

And now this poor lad, the worst they'd ever had probably, was still just a number. The name they'd been given, Burroughs, had been crossed off the register now, and he had been given another wrist tag. She still caught herself thinking of the name, because you couldn't really think of a person as only a number, but knowing it was not the right name made the name itself seem like a ghost. It was even a ghostly-sounding name: 'Burroughs'. A sad sort of name, a name you whispered. She imagined that it belonged to a real person, probably another pilot. Perhaps Burroughs was a friend of the burnt boy who for a brief while had inadvertently borrowed his name. Perhaps he knew nothing about it, and was on leave somewhere, eating bacon and eggs. Perhaps he was dead.

49

Sister sometimes thought that death would be preferable to the state that most of their patients were in. These young servicemen were in a sort of no-man's-land where neither death nor life could claim them. Seaton Hall was itself a kind of limbo. There was little beyond it save the golf course, and the sandy promontory that stretched to Bellside Landing. It looked out over the unchanging sea in a stubborn solitary sort of way, like a kind of challenge. Some mill-owner had built it in the previous century as a way of making his money remembered, but there couldn't have been much leisure or pleasure in it. Sister thought of some of the big houses in the Hebble valley, where the contact with farmland gave them an air both of familiarity and authority. Some of them had gardens that she had visited before the war, and when she was a girl she and Mary Granger had ridden their bicycles all over the valley, stopping at the village shops for lemonade. She had never liked the headland and the dunes, which seemed bleak to her. There was mile upon mile of flat field, mile upon mile of sand. Seaton Hall, with its long bow-windowed front and granite turrets seemed to belong to such featureless surroundings, making as little effort as necessary to be distinctive. It was too large, and too distant, to have ever seemed anything other than a place of confinement. The patients, when they were well enough, could be wheeled along the front, down the single-track road that ran by the gates of the Hall. But there was nowhere in particular for them to be wheeled to. Sand blew over the road from the dunes, and in both directions road and sand stretched indistinguishably as far as the eye could see. The men wandered aimlessly down to the shore-line in their invalid blue, some with arms rigid across their chests, some hooked or slumped over crutches, as though they were performers in an elaborate charade, stiff figures pacing

50

away from each other like duellists, or small groups standing still among clumps of sea-holly as though waiting for a signal that would set them in motion.

Sometimes a nurse pushing a wheelchair might throw back her head and laugh, or in helping a patient to walk hold an arm closely, looking down at the feet. Occasionally a pair of nurses might walk together on the sands, their starched caps like seabirds about to fly. More often they gathered in a room that had been the Hall's library, which had a coffee urn on a trolley, old leather seats and piles of copies of *Nursing Times*, *Home Journal* and *Woman's Weekly*.

Morag was there, drying her eyes, and being comforted by Phyllis and Connie. The other nurses glanced at them and talked quietly among themselves, draining their cups, and straightening their uniforms before going back on duty. They knew why Morag was upset. It had happened to them and would happen again. It happened all the time.

Sister had told Morag that she had to shave the new boy for his operation that morning.

It had to be someone, and Morag was on duty in the ward. Sister knew what had to be done. Phyllis was on bed-pans. Connie was on sheets. The clean sheets were late. It was all routine. Except that all the duty nurses could see that Sister was agitated.

She said it was a big operation. Sir James had briefed her that morning. Everything had to be completely sterile. In particular, the head had to be meticulously re-shaven and cleaned with surgical spirit, even though it was kept routinely shaved. Sir James was going to section a quadrant of the scalp and forehead, detach and bring it forward like the visor of a helmet to assist in the creation of a new face.

Morag said she came over queer just listening to what Sister told her about the operation. When she actually started the shaving she felt better about it. The burns that 51

were scattered back up the left side of the head, like plumes
of exhaust from the weeping cinder of the ear, made her job
harder. But having something to do allowed her to take a
hold on herself. The dressings on the face were harder to
deal with than those on the head, but she had to clean and
in some places shave right up to the scab. It wasn't the
burns themselves. She had seen all kinds of burns. It was the
complete circular extent of the burning over the face, and
the ominous flatness of the dressing over the face, like a
custard pie, that upset her. The whole face was a scab.

Sister said she had done very well, but half an hour later
Morag burst into tears when Connie asked her if she was
feeling all right.

'It's rotten, Connie,' she sobbed. 'Most of him's all right
except for a fractured shoulder, ribs and wrists. Just burns
upwards from the chest and full in the face. Then they
wheeled him away. He's got beautiful feet.'

Later, when they returned to the Old Library for a
sandwich they learned from one of the senior nurses that
the operation was still in progress.

'No golf for Sir James this afternoon,' said Connie.
'Unless he puts in a few nips and tucks.'

'Oh Connie, how can you?' reproached Morag.

'Whoops,' said Connie. 'Can't speak ill of Sir James, can we?'

'She was only joking,' said Phyllis.

'It isn't something you joke about, is it?' said Morag.

'Sir James is always making jokes,' said Connie. 'It's the
only way you can stay sane in this place.'

But Sir James Fandor was not making jokes. After three
hours in the theatre he could only mutter mild curses at
the ineffectiveness of Bangor's grafts. Billy Busby's work,
of course. There was really nothing to be said for Busby
except that at a certain point, perhaps in a shrug of desper-
ation, he could obscurely recognise his own incompetence

and hand things over to someone who knew what he was doing.

The fellow had crashed somewhere in Snowdonia of all places, and it had been tortuous enough getting him to the C & A Hospital at Bangor, let alone all the way up here to Lancashire. But all Bangor had to do was set the fractures and stop the bleeding. Busby had no business messing about with grafts. He had no foresight, no imagination. It was like forcing in the wrong pieces of a jigsaw puzzle.

In this, the first of many operations, Sir James was proposing to redeem the stamp grafts of Billy Busby with something more adventurous. The skin from the scalp would slide forward and be held in place beneath a plaster of Paris cast. The upper edge of the scalp section was joined with silk sutures to what remained of viable skin beneath the eyes. The eyes, being recessed, had somehow been noticeably less burned. One of the original eyelids could be partly saved. Perhaps even the sight of that eye was recoverable. The lower edge of the scalp section was folded under and sutured to the mucous membrane of the mouth. Mucosal grafts would be necessary in a later operation. Lips were such a problem. Later the skin would be re-opened to receive a composite graft from the ear to create the structure of a nose. As Sir James probed, there was some fresh welling of blood. He burned each minute capillary with his electric needle to stem the bleeding, and reflected that the techniques of plastic surgery, though miraculously advanced in incidentals, had not perhaps essentially changed over the 2500 years since skin grafts were known to have been practised. What would the nasal surgery of those Hindus as reported by the Ayur-Veda have been like? A terrible likelihood of infection, of course, and the most primitive of anaesthetics, but the essential process, of transferring material from one part of the body to another, 53 relying on the mysterious natural power of healing, would have been the same. It was indeed mysterious, even miraculous. When angels were wounded, Milton claimed that the 'etherial substance closed, not long divisible.' But that acceleration of healing was only a slight exaggeration of what was in reality an already extraordinarily speedy process. All the patient needed was patience.

When he was delivered back to the ward, it was as though he had been on a voyage of discovery. He might have been to the moon. In his fresh dressings he was like an anointed Pharaoh, the tubes from the mouth the liquid ropes that kept him moored in oblivion just at the edge of the known world, a lordly creature at the centre of attention, like a god to be sustained in darkness.

The nurses were all in awe of him, but with the privilege of handmaidens. In sedation the shrine of his body was quietly accessible, its limbs were washed, its incoming and outgoing fluids watched like auguries.

Phyllis on night duty in the darkened ward was clutching a mug of cocoa, thinking about the dreadful things that Sid Molyneux had suggested to Jean after the dance at the Savoy. She also had a *Home Journal* open in front of her and could just see the print by the light of her lamp. Her eyes moved automatically from page 16 to page 17 on which a wistful girl with freshly permed hair and a camisole was applying something to one crooked elbow. It could have been pumice. It could have been half a lemon. The article didn't help, because it only spoke about soaking the elbow in Epsom Salts. Did she have rough elbows, Phyllis wondered? Could she possibly, she wondered with alarm as she read on, have dowager's hump? The girl in the illustration didn't appear to have dowager's hump, but the hand belonging to the offered elbow covered the area of her neck with delicately spread fingers in the

54

manner of a shop-window dummy or a ballerina being a swan, so she couldn't really tell. Perhaps dowager's hump was something too terrible to show. It sounded too terrible to be included in 'The Little Things that Count in Beauty', though the cure seemed to be as simple as the cure for rough elbows. There were after all many bad things about the body. You were always learning bad things. Like years ago when Sid Molyneux had taken her on the sands and put her hand in his pocket and the pocket had had no bottom because Sid had cut it off. He had held her hand there, like it or not, and pulled her round with his other hand. She hadn't been able to get away. She put down her cocoa and grasped her elbows, hugging herself and shuddering a little at the memory. Yes, her elbows were a little rough. She must remember the tip about the Epsom Salts.

But it wasn't always what they did that seemed so bad, it was what they said. When Jean had told her what Sid had said, even her repeating the words had seemed shocking. She couldn't even look at Jean after she'd said them, though she'd laughed and tut-tutted and commiserated, and said something or other about what filthy brutes boys were. She'd felt the blood coming to her face and she'd stared hard at the teapot until Jean had asked her if she wanted another cup.

It sometimes seemed to her as if all men must be like that, however prim or proper they might be on the surface. Like Dr Simpson at the Unit party. It wasn't exactly anything he had said or done, just the way he had behaved because his wife wasn't there and because they weren't working. You could tell. She wouldn't even trust Dr Simpson now. Perhaps there was no man you could trust. Like something she had heard in a film once: 'The only Indian I trust is a dead Indian.'

The stillness of the ward made her think of all the patients 55 as interestingly on the borders of death, even though she knew that most of them were in little danger. It was a fantasy entirely possible in the depth of the night. The green light over the door at the end of the ward glowed dimly like an explorer's torch illuminating an inaccessible cave full of votive treasure that could never be disturbed. Sometimes she had quickly to suppress her fantasies before she terrified herself. What if all the men were somehow to wake at once and rise from their beds and make demands of her? During the day they were only what she knew they were: damaged boys, immobilised for the most part, helpless and in pain. At night a spirit of male adventure slumbered with them, an invulnerable daemon with a drive to face the unfaceable, ready to stir and wake, to take on again the imperfect human shapes that it compelled to do its bidding. Words were sometimes shouted out in sleep, incoherent warnings and challenges that broke the sunken stillness of the ward and startled her from her reveries; intimate moans that hovered between tenderness and pain; wild laughter. Then all would be as suddenly still again.

Phyllis tried the exercises suggested by the *Home Journal* for improving the bust-line, then thought she had better do them standing up, stood up, and then felt foolish although there was no one to see her. Instead, she walked slowly down the ward.

As she walked past the bed of the new boy she thought she saw his foot shift beneath the sheet. She looked at her watch: almost time to give him another injection. She wasn't frightened of 'Burroughs' as Morag and some of the other nurses were. He was so helpless. Patched and swathed like that, he seemed without personality. You couldn't be frightened of that blank shape. She was sometimes frightened of eyes, and grins, and reaching hands. But 'Burroughs' couldn't hurt her. He could only be pitied.

When she came to give him the injection she wondered if his breathing was a bit irregular. As she sat by his bed preparing the needle, it seemed that from his bandages, from the appalling slit that was his mouth, there came an irregular wheezing. She leaned forward to listen.

At her pressure against the edge of the bed, his arm moved slightly against the front of her body, displaced by the shifted angle of the mattress. It gave her a start, but she let it rest there.

What was this odd sound coming from the slit in his dressing, this intermittent but determined expulsion of air? Was it a death rattle? A clearing of the throat? It was faint, but weirdly rhythmical, like the sound of a band carried by the wind from villages away, when only the tiny percussive thumps survive the chance journey, and the tune is lost.

The arm moved again, and it moved of its own accord. It was tense with an acknowledgment of her nearness and with the containment of pain. Phyllis's hands busied themselves with the injection and its blessing: it poured into his body as if in response to the desperate distracting mantra that his mind had learned to cling to and which was half-voicing in his throat. She could not know it, but the ghastly sounds were an approximation of the music that for much of the time had been all he had to cling to, the immortal Bix:

> 'And doesn't that smell like ham and eggs?
> No, that smells like bacon and eggs.
> Bacon and eggs? Ham and eggs?
> Oh gee!'

As the needle did its divine work, once more he relapsed into unconsciousness.

7

If Robbo came round after tea, they would go out and play. Granny didn't mind him going down to the promenade if he was with someone else, though she didn't like him going alone. When they were on the sands, with the tide far out, Robbo would go berserk, running full tilt with his arms outstretched, uttering bestial moans. The sand was sculpted by the retreated waters into hard wave-like corrugations, stretching as far as the eye could see. David hardly liked to spoil their perfection as he trod, although he knew that the tide re-established the pattern effortlessly each day. Robbo, however, gashed and scuffed the sand as he swooped and turned, leaving shuffled paths in imitation of the vapour trail of a damaged Spitfire.

Further out, near the tideline and even beyond, were solitary figures bent for bait, or standing at a distance from an orbiting dog. The evening sun cast stilts beneath them on the glistening shore.

The dipping sun was like a challenge to the ocean to capture its light. The sea had retreated to the horizon, like a fielder running to the boundary for a carelessly lobbed ball, and its waters reflected a dazzling glow of premature triumph. The sun reddened. It did not seem to sink so much as come nearer. It hung, enlarged, upon the edge of the sky, lighting up the coast from St Peter's to Bellside Landing.

Bellside Landing!

To David this remote and unvisited limit of the coast was more than the place of ancient and urgent departure that its name suggested. On the contrary, for some reason it seemed to him a place of conclusion and repose. It was a place to get to, rather than to leave from. But how did one get to it? Beyond the last tram stop, where the concrete of the tram shelter was cracked and choked with weeds, the dunes began. And they stretched for miles and miles, longer than any picnic walk, endless drifted hillocks of fine white sand combed with reedy tufts of grass, and broken sea-holly. David could hardly believe that the dunes did not go on for ever.

Robbo was always keen to wander in the other direction, towards the world of deckchair attendants, ice-cream, the vast rusted supports of the North Pier and its interior like the dank nave of an iron church. The further south they went, the greater the likelihood of organised pleasure: at each point where they might remount the steps to the promenade and cross the tramlines, there was a fresh opportunity. After the small hotels of the North Shore, each with its distinctive name in gilded lettering against the red brick, came the tea-rooms and ice-cream parlours. Then the tourist shops, the fish-and-chips, the side-shows. At the centre of town, where the trams diverged, began the more dignified and civic mysteries: the ballroom, the circus, the superior South Pier with its theatre. And beyond, stretching an equivalent distance, it seemed, to the dunes of the north, was the Palace of Pleasure, a lavish acreage of concrete, with coloured domes and soaring white railway tracks. If Bellside Landing was a haven, the 59

Palace of Pleasure was a busy junction of the spirit. That grown-ups were known to flock there presented it as a place of secret transformations, its terrors ritualised, its circuits in reality unconfined by mere geography. Its most notable possession, set at its very portals, was a blind-windowed house decorated with nodding creatures and echoing with vile mechanical laughter that appeared to come from a ginger-bearded tar in a glass case. What went on in this building, evidently misnamed the House of Fun, David never discovered. But the laughter echoed in his nightmares.

At evening, many of these fascinating places seemed to be closing the moment they could reach them. Those that were coming to life required money, tickets, unlimited time, adulthood; or were, finally, too distant.

Robbo said that they must see the mermaid. He had heard his brother talking about the mermaid. She was in a tank on South Shore, and she was alive.

'She's got no clothes on, either,' he said.

'How much is it?' asked David.

'Dunno,' said Robbo. 'It might be a shilling.'

'A shilling!' said David.

'Well, maybe not,' said Robbo. 'But we'd better start saving.'

'Will they let us in if she's got no clothes on?'

'Why not?' said Robbo. 'Mermaids don't wear clothes anyway. Ever seen a mermaid with a pair of knickers on?'

It wasn't easy to save up. It was already impossible to decide between *Radio Fun* and the *Dandy*, and often David bought both. And then there was Mrs Tewkins. Whenever they were hot or bored they would say: 'Let's go to Mrs Tewkins!'

You could buy ice-cream from Mrs Tewkins at about
60 half the price of shop ice-cream, two scoops for a penny.

You had to take your own container. She would fill a small mixing bowl for sixpence, and once she filled David's kitchen cup up to the brim and higher for his penny just so that she could clean out the machine. It was quite a small machine. It was packed with salt, and you turned a handle like a churn.

Although generous, Mrs Tewkins was a silent and un-smiling woman. She was of a size that made Granny and even Mrs Thesiger seem elegant, and she was strangely heedless of her barrel-like appearance. Quite often she shuffled to her outhouse in a housecoat that she had not bothered to do up. You rang the front doorbell and if she saw you were holding a teacup she simply nodded to you to go round the side. Then she reappeared in the yard, sometimes holding the housecoat together in front of her corseted body, sometimes not.

But she deposited the scoops of ice-cream with liberal hand.

A direct contrast to the stout ladies of Viewforth Road and sometimes fearsomely to be seen there, was the Witch. Although she was thought to live some distance away in Bennet Avenue, she nearly always seemed to be making some new and angular journey in the local streets. She was always alone, and always not quite convincingly enough going anywhere. Her route seemed to take her at a tangent to any likely purpose.

Robbo was keen to pursue her at a safe distance, like an Indian scout. David was doubtful: he thought it would be wrong, and he was afraid. But when Jean heard them talking about her, she shuddered.

'Is she still around?' she said. 'That old bag?'

She told them how the Witch used to shake her umbrella at her and Phyllis, and how David's mother had once seen her pick up a gob from the pavement and eat it.

61

'A what?' cried Robbo incredulously.

'A gob. You know,' said Jean. 'A gob of phlegm. All thick and yellow like an egg yolk.'

The two boys groaned and retched theatrically, and ran off up Viewforth Road and through the alley, looking for the Witch again.

Robbo asked David when his father was coming home on leave. David didn't know how to answer this question. He didn't even know if he wanted to, or was intended to, answer it. Robbo asked it in his least friendly manner, and David knew that if they had not been alone it might have turned into a form of inquisition. But he also felt guilty in some obscure way because his father didn't turn up on leave. Robbo's father did. He was to be seen quite often in the Robinson kitchen with an air of lordly relaxation, eating enormous meals, or smoking and staring into space. Robbo said that his mother started saving up coupons the minute he left on a Sunday night so that she would have plenty of meat and eggs to feed him when he came again. Mr Robinson, who was a corporal in the Royal Engineers and had been at Dunkirk, was a bad-tempered man with bulging eyes. David was amazed at how angry he got at quite unimportant things like the newspaper not being folded back, so that bits of it ended up in different places. He seemed to get particularly angry with Robbo, which was very unfair when you thought about it, seeing that he had shut off his fingers in the car. David would have been quite interested to see the car, and to look at the precise place by the door-catch where the fingers had come off, but Robbo said that the car had been put away for the duration, and he didn't want to show him. David wondered if the fingers had dropped off there and then, and how much it had hurt, but he never dared to ask.

62   Robbo, however, asked all kinds of questions.

'I expect your dad's got somewhere else to go to when he gets leave, hasn't he?'

It was the sort of question that suggested a possible truth that David had not contemplated before. But there was a sort of answer.

'We lived in London. He doesn't really live here.'

'Well, why do you live here, then?'

'It's just so as my Granny can look after me, isn't it?'

'And are you sure he's a pilot?'

David had once made such a claim. He couldn't now remember why he had needed to, except that Robbo was the sort of person who required to be impressed or he became easily bored, and once he was bored he was likely to be hostile.

'He's going to bomb Germany soon.'

'Get away.'

'Yes. Give them some of their own medicine.'

David knew that Robbo would give him trouble on this score. Sure enough, at the earliest opportunity he called out to Miss Mackie in front of the class, without even raising his hand:

'Miss! David says his father's a fighter pilot!'

'That's a very fine thing to be, George, but you mustn't interrupt.'

'I bet he isn't,' said Toffee Mynors.

'Sydney, that's enough,' said Miss Mackie. 'Be quiet.'

After the class, Phillie Lacey came up to David in the corridor. She was a small girl with reddish hair, who usually wore a hand-knitted green cardigan. She was very quiet in class and never talked unless Miss Mackie asked her a question, and even then she might not say anything.

'My dad was a pilot,' she said. 'We've got a medal.'

David felt ashamed, but he told himself that he didn't 63

know that his father was not a pilot. He now knew that there were many different occupations in the RAF, some of them having nothing to do with aircraft, but his father *did* have something to do with Lancaster bombers. That much he knew. It was surely possible that he flew them. He brought to school a little metal knife that his father had sent him, made out of a propeller. But he kept it in his satchel all day, and didn't produce it in class. Had he really understood correctly that it was made out of a propeller? How could such a small thing, its blade made of pale dull pitted metal, its handle of rings of other kinds of metal threaded on, and bolted, he made out of something as large as a propeller? Unlikely as its history was, David was suddenly seized by the realisation that a pilot would have no leisure or opportunity to make such a thing, nor the tools. He had seen a film, where the young heroes ate cake and lounged around in their heavy flying jackets in huts on the edge of the airfield. One of them had whittled a piece of wood and made jokes which annoyed the others. He happened to be the first one to be killed, too, and everyone was sorry. But whittling a piece of wood was not the same as this piece of ornamental engineering, and David could not see his father as a daredevil, a figure of idle fun.

He didn't even show the paper-knife to Phillie Lacey.

The summer was coming to an end, and soon the last holidaymakers would have gone home. David hung around the bathroom when Jacko was shaving. He watched him peer into the mirror as he worked up the lather in his shaving bowl, drawing down his upper lip over his teeth and peering down his nose. David laughed.

'Are you pretending to be a monkey?'

'Get away.'

64 Jacko shaved very slowly and carefully as though

performing a surgical operation on a meringue. David looked at the opening of his pyjama bottoms.

'You're showing a light, Jacko,' he said. 'Don't you know there's a war on?'

'What are you on about?'

'Your curtains aren't closed properly.'

Jacko looked down and tugged his pyjamas across his body so that the knot of the pyjama cord stood out at his hip.

'Cheeky little sod,' he said, returning to the scrutiny of his chin.

David felt immune so long as the precariously achieved foam glued Jacko's face to the bathroom mirror.

'What's the matter with your jimmy, Jacko,' he said with pretended concern. 'It looks all sore.'

At this, Jacko came at David with a razor, howling, and David retreated down the landing. Jacko returned to the mirror.

'Jacko,' said David, from the doorway.

'What now?' said Jacko. 'You're a pest, you are.'

'Shall we go and see the mermaid?'

'What mermaid?'

'The mermaid down South Shore, in a glass case,' explained David. 'Robbo says she's in the nicky-nude.'

'In the nicky-nude?' said Jacko, scornfully. 'I don't believe you.'

'That's what Robbo said,' replied David. 'Shall we go?'

'What would I want to go down South Shore for, to see a mermaid in the nicky-nude?' said Jacko. 'I don't have to pay to see a girl in the nicky-nude.'

He wiped his face dry with the towel, and splashed toilet water on his cheeks.

'Have you seen Sylvia Elswick in the nicky-nude?' asked David, emboldened by the depth of the conversation.

65

'Get away,' repeated Jacko with infinite weariness. He applied toilet water under his arms, hunching each shoulder as he did so.

'That looks just like a monkey,' said David, himself squatting and bouncing and scratching his armpits.

'I'm coming to deal with you when I've done my exercises,' said Jacko, closing the door on him. 'You'd better try to find somewhere to hide, but you won't be able to because I'll find you wherever you are.'

'You're better-looking than Spencer Tracey,' called out David through the keyhole in pacification. A thudding noise was coming from the bathroom.

'That doesn't take,' panted Jacko, 'much doing.'

In the end, though, Jacko went with David to see the mermaid. Sylvia was with them, but at the last minute she hung back.

'I'll wait for you out here,' she said.

'Aren't you coming in, then?' asked Jacko.

'I don't think I really want to,' she said.

'Perhaps you'd better not,' said Jacko. 'It might give you ideas.'

Sylvia looked at Jacko reproachfully, and gave him a little push with the heel of her hand. David had never seen a push that looked less like a push.

'You aren't half unfriendly these days, Jacko,' she said. 'I don't know what's got into you, I really don't.'

'What did I say?' laughed Jacko, appealing to David. 'Tell me what I said.'

'I'll be in there, having a cup of tea,' she said, appeasingly, touching the lapel of his jacket. She indicated a café a little way down the street. 'You can tell me what it was like, if you want, but I just don't feel like seeing something like that.'

She smiled sadly, and walked away.

'Something like what?' spluttered Jacko to her retreating figure. He turned to David. 'We don't know what it's like yet, do we?'

They discovered soon enough what it was like.

It was a woman in a tank of water. You couldn't really say whether she was wearing any clothes or not, unless you counted a rather coarse-haired long blonde wig that hid a very great deal of the upper half of her body. Below the waist she was under water, and there was a cunning little fountain trickling right next to her that made it impossible to see if she was wearing anything. A fin came out of the water in the corner of the tank, stirring slowly as though moved by a revolving piece of clockwork. You couldn't look through the side of the tank, only from above, and the lights were placed in such a way that you could never quite discount the ripples made by the fountain in order to see the precise nature of the shape beneath.

Nobody else seemed to be at all disappointed. David looked at Jacko, who was staring at the woman as though he had never been three or four feet from a pair of bare shoulders before. The woman seemed quite unconcerned, looking ahead, her mouth occasionally moving slightly as though she didn't want anyone to see that she was chewing. She might have been staring into a fire or having her hair done.

A somnolent crab on some rocks in the corner started to edge its way towards her.

'Hey, watch out, missus,' a little boy shouted. 'It could give you quite a pinch, that.'

'So could I and all,' said an older voice. Everybody laughed.

David wandered off into the permanent exhibition at the end of the hall, and into a dusty room up some steps   67 at the back. He couldn't think why there was no one there. It was much more interesting. There were photographs of real freaks, like the Mule-faced Woman. David couldn't imagine what had gone wrong with their faces, and why it didn't go wrong with people more often. He didn't want to look at the photographs. There were some other things like bits of farm machinery, with a sign revealing that they were instruments of torture. There was a mummified skeleton propped up in one corner. It had a sign saying: 'Jo-Jo, the Dried-Up Man.' Patches of matted woolly hair still adhered to the scalp. The eyelids were shut but concave, the nose crudely collapsed like a dud ping-pong ball. The body was the colour of soil. Dried-up he might be, but there was no mistaking that he was a man. It stood from the groove formed by his knock-kneed withered legs like a broken suitcase handle. David was suddenly distracted by a sound from the only living exhibit in the room. In the opposite corner was something like a parrot's cage, with a sign above it saying: 'The Largest Maggot in the World.' The maggot, totally covered in something that might have been grey skin or grey silky fur, was pulsing and flexing in the sand at the bottom of the cage. It was the size of a small animal. David did not look at it for long, but soon ran back down the steps to the front of the hall where the mermaid's tank stood. Jacko had already left.

In the café they were both drinking tea, and Sylvia looked as though she had been crying. Jacko wasn't being nearly as interested in her as he had been in the mermaid.

On the way home, David tried to cheer them up. He told them about Jo-Jo, the Dried-Up Man and the Largest Maggot in the World. They took a tram, clanking in silence along the tramway between the low concrete walls made in sections designed like gates or flags. Then they walked up Dawson Avenue.

'I know,' said David. 'Let's go to Mrs Tewkins.'

But they didn't want to go to Mrs Tewkins. Sylvia went straight home. She said her mother was expecting her for tea as her Aunt Madge was coming. David and Jacko went on to Number 20 and into the kitchen, where Jacko made himself a piece of bread and jam.

'Don't I get any?' asked David.

'Can't you make it yourself?' said Jacko.

Jacko was inconsolable, but David didn't know exactly what was wrong. He stood by the sink, letting the cold water run and staring out into the back yard. Granny and Jean came in from the front room to get the tea, so David and Jacko were made to help. It was Saturday, and they were having tinned salmon. Usually Jacko would have disappeared straight after tea without helping to clear up, announcing his departure with his usual brevity. But he lingered in his seat, even stacking a few plates and handing them to Jean to be taken away. He kept his cup filled, and sat at the table reading the newspaper.

Later that night, when David went to bed, Jacko was in his room with his radio on. David washed his face and brushed his teeth, and then lingered in the doorway of Jacko's room before going upstairs.

'Have you ever been to Bellside Landing, Jacko?' he asked.

Jacko was just lying on his bed, with his clothes on. He wasn't even reading.

'No,' said Jacko.

'I expect Sylvia would like to go to Bellside Landing,' said David. 'Couldn't we all go? Take a picnic?'

'No,' said Jacko.

'Did you like that mermaid, Jacko?' said David.

'No,' said Jacko.

'You couldn't see nothing, though, could you, Jacko?' 69

JOHN FULLER

'Not a bloody thing,' said Jacko.

'You should have seen that Jo-Jo the Dried-Up Man,' said David. 'You should have seen his jimmy. It was even bigger than yours.'

'Unlikely,' said Jacko.

'That maggot, though,' went on David with a shudder of remembrance. 'Do you think it *was* a maggot? I mean, it couldn't really have been a maggot, could it?'

'Perhaps it was a jimmy,' said Jacko. He didn't seem inclined to make out a serious case for it.

Jacko and Sylvia made it up after a few days, though. One night David woke up and needed a drink of water. His cup was full of dirty painting water so he had to tiptoe all the way down to the kitchen, where there might after all even be something to eat. As he passed silently through the hall, treading only on the blue shapes of the carpet (which was hard to do as there were fewer of them than any other) he heard a noise from the lounge. He thought everyone was asleep, and was puzzled. It sounded like an animal eating something. He didn't know whether to go on to the kitchen or back upstairs. Then it seemed like voices, and he thought that perhaps Granny hadn't switched the radio off. He looked through the keyhole. The sideboard lamp must have been left on, because he could see a little hole-shaped picture of the end of the settee and what must have been Sylvia and Jacko holding something on Jacko's knee. *Was* it an animal? He couldn't see very well. It was mostly hands. And now he could just hear them laughing and whispering. He was about to turn the door-knob and see what they had found in there, when they were suddenly quiet. He must have made a noise outside the door. They knew he was there and didn't want him. He suddenly felt frightened, not of any intruder or a ghost or an animal, but frightened of Jacko and Sylvia

70

and what they were doing in there in the lamp-light when everyone was asleep. He tiptoed back upstairs again with as big strides as he could manage without creaking, and forgot all about his glass of water.

Later that week Jacko's call-up papers came.

At night, just before he fell asleep, David used to think about Jacko going off to be a soldier, and about Jacko and Sylvia. The more he thought about Sylvia the more he thought that she was very nice. Really she was nicer than Jacko. It wasn't just that she was *nice*. He thought about the way she put a sweet in her mouth. At the moment it went in, at that precise moment, her eyes couldn't actually see it, but her eyes weren't looking anywhere else. Her mouth paused before it began to suck, as though to prepare itself seriously for the flavour. Perhaps she would take him on an expedition to Bellside Landing. Or perhaps if his father came back on leave they could all go.

They left the light on the stairs for him. He could always hear voices coming from downstairs as he went to sleep, because he left the attic door open. He thought of sleep as disembodied, like sound or light; something that might pass up the stairs by the grandfather clock and pause outside his bedroom. It slowed everything down. It was like something waiting for him.

8

Waking turned into a more regular process, and as it did so became less bewildering but more frustrating. He knew that waking should be completed by the act of opening the eyelids to the light. It was a liberation from the dark foolishness of dreams, where one self-indulgence bred another without interference from reality. But waking now was a constriction of the freedom of sleep, emerging into the cruel restraint of the head and its frustrated entrances. Everything seemed to be concentrated into that limiting tight wall behind the face. He felt shut into it. There was nowhere else to go.

It was worse when the dressings were first removed, for his eyelids would not obey his injunction to move them. It was not surprising, for they were hardly his eyelids. They lay heavy as pillows on his eyes. Moved for him by Dr Simpson, the action sent no helpful messages to the surviving muscles. It was like someone moving his ears. But gradually he became accustomed to what the action revealed, a movement, or kind of grey shifting within his head that he could not control with his mind. He knew it was light, and therefore that the shapes that it began to make belonged to the outside world.

Adjusting to these unguessable pictures seemed no stranger than adjusting to the weight and distance of immovable and half-movable objects. Simply sitting up seemed an adventure.

And yet so much was expected of him. He knew what was expected. That was how he was different from a baby, who did not know; but in other respects his coming to consciousness was like being born, and its being accompanied by full-time female attention was entirely appropriate.

He knew all the nurses by the shape of their shoulders and the timbre of their voices. He connected the voices with different degrees of gentleness. They were so much the bearings of his existence that he had no time to think about their attitudes to himself. The passage from shock to rehabilitation, reiterated through dozens of operations, allowed no self-consciousness. It was a limbo of endurance without the opportunity for memory or prospect. He could not speak, and could barely entertain speech. Procedures were explained, and simple questions were put to the muffled turbulence at the side of his head that was his hearing, but he felt that the whole of the rational world had dwindled in effect to the manipulation of his face. This manipulation had no need to explain itself, or to seek corroboration. It had become almost like a natural process. It did not need his fear or approval, just as his forgotten past did not need his love or apology. Whatever history he had left behind on the Welsh mountain was as effectively destroyed as the aircraft he had been flying. It was replaced by an eternal present of careful hands, starched uniform fronts, face powder, words of encouragement.

It seemed to him vaguely like an answer to something, as though the familiarity of these female bodies, indirectly encountered as they were, echoed his familiarity with   73 them in some alternative or hypothetical existence. They, however, identified themselves by name, and he could not give them his name. He was drawn into their world, the helpless centre of it. And yet they had come together to enter his world, whatever they might be, and were the willing servants of it. Whatever life they had was not only unknown to him but quite beyond his speculation.

Perhaps if he could remember his name, or be bothered to remember it, it would bring illumination. He did not think so.

The talkative one who felt bony when he leaned on her was called Connie. The one with smooth arms who didn't mind putting them anywhere around his body to hoist him about was called Phyllis. The one who didn't talk much was called Morag.

Why could he remember their names and not his own? He had heard one of them refer to him as 'Burroughs', but he did not think that that was his name. Why didn't he care what his name was? Did he care or not?

It didn't seem to matter what his name was. His identity had been stolen. It was like a masquerade where he had no particular role to play, only the absence of a role. He was certainly not going to play the role of 'Burroughs', whoever he was. He was simply crammed into a simulacrum of his own nature, tightly bound into a collapsed shape, an unrecognisable half-mobile puppet. He was like a spent bullet, a struck match.

Why should he allow himself to be fed by these girls when he should be making love to them? When his body was absolutely out of his control they had kept it idling, turning it, watching it, sponging it, injecting it. It was their duty, but they must have done it with a kind of love. He was content to continue under their care. It was perhaps, in a strange sort of way, his own duty. If this was his destiny it was still a part of his duty; of his duties. These enduring agonies, the operations, were not misnamed: they were no different from his earlier operations, the 'ops' that took him from the airfield out over the Channel, masked and elated, to face unknown dangers.

Once tempered and intermittent, pain became something that he could contemplate, usually with nausea or resentment. To that extent it was worse than when it was continuous and when there was no escape from it. When he had been the pain, when he had simply been the present embodiment of its blind purposes, his mind was of as little use as a moth fluttering against a candle. Now, as the anaesthetics could take a reasonable and regular hold, and healing ran its magic course, the mind discovered intervals in which it could gather its funds of rage and fear. In those intervals, too, the mind reflected on what it was. He had never before felt less at one with his body. He felt perplexed by sometimes not quite knowing what his body was. For much of his life he had more or less thought that his body was permanent and indestructible, his mind the beneficent monarch of an absolutely loyal kingdom. Now that his body had not only proved that it could die by coming so close to death but had also shown how easily it could be blotted out in its most essential features, that loyalty became a hollow charade. The mind, as a result, stood under arraignment, charged with claiming a false authority. Mental autocracy was a sham. The king was a citizen like any other.

But the pain was a sign of his resistance, his stubborn refusal to abdicate. He couldn't give up. He couldn't trust the physical process. If he gave up, his whole body might collapse into its constituent matter, a general sloughing like the shapeless healing granulation of hopelessly damaged flesh. The mind's idea of identity must surely be the   75 force that shapes the body. Pain is the echo of that force's surveillance of its kingdom, news of revolt in its provinces. But why should we require identity at all if it is dependent on such division?

If this was healing, he'd be better off dead. It was pushing him further and further into isolation.

For one thing, the forgetfulness was no passing whim of the distracted mind as it lurched erratically back into its function of control. It so completely hid his private past from him that he might have drawn his first breath at Biggin Hill watching Chris Crawford feed the stove with tins of floor polish to get it decently alight. He tried to work on memories like these, to snowball them backwards into a narrative of his life: Crawford skating on dusters to polish the floor, Crawford with his thick finger in the manual, inventing obscene acronyms for procedures that later were to assist in their undoing when there was never time to observe them by the book. He could think forward well enough, and he remembered how Crawford had died. He could remember the whole litany of the dead: Crawford, Silver, Driven, Stike, Blondworm, Rogers, Jauncey, Price, Leverbarrow, Headlong, Lacey, Beskett.

'I'm like a walking bloody war memorial,' he thought. 'And I can't even walk.'

But soon he began to be able to use his eye, and he stopped stumbling into every bed or chair in the ward. He could walk round and round the table in the recreation room with one hand trailing lightly on it, touching the corners occasionally as if to make sure that it was really there.

'What's he thinking about?' Morag would ask Phyllis, and Phyllis would shrug.

'It gets on my nerves,' said Connie. 'It's like a caged
76 lion.'

He was trying to think back beyond the noisy theatre of the sky, beyond the roll-call of the dead, getting nowhere. His tiny past was peopled with players who had no past themselves, no childhoods, no relations. Anything distinctive about them belonged only to their interaction with one another, whatever gave them appreciable character in the mess. They might have been sketched for an epic poem. They were like grinning anonymous faces in a group photograph.

And yet they too had been real people, whom the war had brought together to destroy. Beskett, who would crack his fingers together. Lacey, who was always reading. Headlong, eager to organise cricket. Leverbarrow, combing his black hair. Price, short of money. Jauncey, with unpleasant stories about his sister. Rogers, whom no one ever noticed. Blondworm, an object of amazement in the showers. Stike, already trained as an accountant. Driven, who managed to conceal and feed a pair of labradors. Silver, the keep-fit fiend. Crawford, with his gramophone.

It was Crawford who played the Bix Beiderbecke records that still endlessly jogged in his brain. Bix Beiderbecke and his Gang playing 'At the Jazz Band Ball'. Lots of Frank Trumbauer numbers. Bix playing solo piano in 'In a Mist'. And above all the immortal Broadway Bellhops with 'There Ain't No Land Like Dixieland To Me', with Bix on cornet, and Joe Venuti on violin, and the vocal by Irving Kaufman:

'Hey, tell me, doesn't that look like Dixieland?
Sure that looks like Dixieland . . .'

Chris had been given his gramophone when he was thirteen by his Uncle Charlie. The records had come with it, and he had hardly anything more recent. Dance bands left him cold.

'You don't hear the instruments,' he would say. 'They've got no freedom.'

The others would groan, and Driven once produced some Glenn Miller records. But Chris Crawford would play nothing but Bix.

These memories were almost as precise as the position of the instruments in the cockpit, but they derived from nothing. They had no earlier associations. They were like a completely contained world, as though someone had written them for a play, or invented them as the Spitfire had had to be invented. And they were as impermanent. All these airmen were dead.

It seemed extraordinary that he was not dead, too. At times he felt that he carried with him nothing but the jaunty residue of all the lives of his friends, pared away into the bright repetitive nostalgia of the tune he most remembered:

> 'Is there any place so nice?
> Do I have to ask you twice?
> Yes, sir! Yes, sir! That's my paradise!'

Perhaps if he could forget the tune he could remember who he really was.

Dr Simpson said it would be a matter of time, but he didn't feel that this could be right. Time was something he suffered. How could it be a cure?

He should be somewhere else! He felt he was missing something, or perhaps someone was missing him. It was like having obtusely chosen his fate instead of suffering it, having chosen it out of defiance, to spite someone. Time conspired to isolate this feeling. Constrained by time, the restlessness increased even though there was no relief for it. It was nothing frantic. There was nothing to be glimpsed that offered hope of escape. It was only a kind of drawn-out wild deadened feeling, a kind of sublime boredom. Time never passes; you can only say that time has passed. So he never knew where it might lead him. He could only wait. And the waiting, which had become his whole condition of life, was frustratingly boring.

He longed to eat proper food: bacon, Marmite, kidneys. He imagined their individual smells. They seemed as exact and impossible as his dead companions. A steak was as legendary as Hector dragged around the walls of Troy, a kipper as fantastic as Plantagenet politics. But he still had to feed through a straw. Dr Simpson had explained their particular difficulty with the mouth. They had repeatedly to regraft in order to fight the natural contracture around the mouth. The condition was known as microstoma, and it became, perhaps unreasonably, the focus of his anguish about his face. Microstoma, 'little mouth'. It sounded, and felt, like a disastrous constriction, a fatal closing of the major communication of the organism with the sustaining world.

Plugged to the nipple, the mouth learns ingestion. Food is the animal's contact with the planet, whose cycle of growth is designed to make planetary matter accessible to an organism that is nothing more itself than a peculiar arrangement of planetary matter. This shrinking of the burnt mouth, seeming to threaten an unimaginable closure, was therefore like the shrivelling of a plant's root. It was as if he himself were being cropped for some purpose. And that purpose was non-existent. It was accident. It was waste. Men and women were so many weeds, expendable isolated clones of a central organism that was content enough to exist in the mass and could afford to lose the superfluity.

'It's doing very well, you'll be glad to hear,' said Dr Simpson. 'We shall soon be ready for the mucosal grafts 79 to reconstruct the vermilion of the lips. Sir James gets back from Scotland next week. I think he'll be very pleased.'

Sometimes after his sessions with the doctors he wanted to weep, but that was one of the things his face wouldn't do. All this care, this microscopic attention, the conferences, the theory, the hours in the operating theatre. They might have been planning a secret weapon. The War Cabinet could not have worked longer hours. And all for him.

It broke him up inside with gratitude and disbelief, and at the same time he thought it useless. If he was simply one of millions of perimetral nodes of the abstract human organism, a minor point of damage, there could be no absolute virtue in repairing him, any more than there would be in stemming the evaporation of a lake or the dispersal of a cloud by preserving the positions of the molecules at its shifting boundaries. The signals he sent out as a damaged nodal point were presumably designed as a warning to the organism and felt as pain by himself, but the pity of society and the techniques of Seaton Hall seemed to him no more significant than the blind rescue by ants of one of their trodden number, or the alerted routines of the cells themselves in the natural process of healing. It would happen. It was designed to happen. But not because he was a significant individual.

And yet the pain he bore was his own pain. It was no one else's. He could almost think it was beautiful, the psychic print of the strangest process in the world: the lapsing of the organism into the inorganic. No one else felt it. He could only transmit it as a message for the perimeter, just as it was transmitted to his own brain from the terminals of his nerves.

It was nearly Christmas when he first thought he could see Phyllis's face clearly enough to see it as a face.

It seemed a pleasant enough face, the more agreeable for directing its gaze at his own. He soon discovered that most people looked away. The doctors of course looked closely. Their purely scientific attention allowed him to scan their own faces without the trouble of fielding the difficult emotional signals that usually came from faces, especially when they were that close. When Dr Simpson peered into his good eye with a calibrated instrument held like a gun, he could not help being reminded of the gunsights of his Hurricane. The doctor was a lonely explorer like the pilot, building not destroying. But he understood why doctors wore masks. The facelessness was appropriate, because the face is the agent of social interaction. The pilot has to become like a machine, just like the doctor.

He knew, though, that he could not be a pilot again. The question was, could he become a man again? One day he tried to ask Phyllis this question, but finding a way to put it was just as hard as actually speaking the words, because his mouth still didn't quite behave in the way he wanted it to.

'Is it,' his mouth said separately, 'very bad?'

They were negotiating the steps down into the sun-room where the irregular chopping sound of a table tennis ball told them that time was passing amiably. Phyllis didn't reply. What could she say? But she held his arm a little tighter and rested her head for a moment on his shoulder in acknowledgment both of the question and her own involvement in the impossible subject it attempted to raise.

81

9

Jill Simpson didn't shut the door when she went to the toilet. She went on talking, weaving pipe-cleaners with her pale fingers, as she walked down the passage to the bathroom. David followed, listening. He always seemed to be listening when he was with Jill. She liked to give him things to do.

She gave him the pipe-cleaners to hold, and David saw that it was a little lamb on long bent legs.

She sat on the wooden seat with her knickers collapsed around her ankles. She was wearing sandals whose cut-out leather revealed lozenges of white sock partly obscured by the knickers.

David was hardly listening to what she was saying. It was something about her uncle. For him it was entirely drowned by the tinkle beneath her. Her skirt was bunched up and as she leaned forward she raised and lowered her feet, pointing her sandalled toes and nodding at them as she talked.

'Don't look,' she said suddenly. 'I'm going to do number twos.'

And even as she spoke, glaring at him, the glare turned to a mere abstracted frown. She seemed to stare right through him. Her mouth deepened and strained in concentration.

David turned his head as instructed, wondering if he should now take up the conversation. Since he hadn't been listening properly, he could hardly do so. He studied a picture on the bathroom wall. It showed a beached fishing-boat in moonlight, covered with nets. Jill was making a tiny straining sound, and he wondered, too late he knew, if he should have gone out of the room altogether. The moment quite abruptly took on a unique and almost ceremonious formality. The moon was lodged on its side. The nets were drying, even though the boat had been upturned, as if at the end of the season. David was holding the lamb in both hands, like some kind of offering.

There was a deep plop, followed by the rustle of paper, and a rich smell whose outrageousness seemed to be licensed by the bland confidence of her social manners.

'It's all right,' said Jill. 'You can look now.'

He looked, and she was wiping herself.

A lot of the time she talked about her party. She was going to have one guest for each year of her age. This relatively small number still seemed quite large to David, who did not have parties. David, indeed, did not have friends to tea in the ceremonious way that Jill did, for if Robbo happened to turn up he would thieve bread and jam as Jacko did. The idea of collecting plates of home-made biscuits and glasses of milk from the kitchen and carefully carrying them elsewhere would have seemed bizarre. There was no system for receiving guests at Viewforth Road, certainly not one that David had access to. In fact, Jill had never been home with him, and he would not think of asking her. It didn't even occur to him to wonder why he did not think of asking her. He accepted his role as a satellite. Surely she would not want to come round. 83

His invitation to the party had been written out by Mrs Simpson on a card with rounded corners in an old-fashioned lettering of a kind that he had seen in church notices. She had used a pale green ink, which somehow was like the clothes she wore. The weight and authority of the card almost frightened him, and at the same time seemed like a privilege. It was like an invitation from the whole Simpson family, an elegant summons.

He was surprised to discover that no one else in his class except Phillie Lacey had received one. He could not imagine who the other guests were going to be. He put his invitation between the pages of the *King George V Empire Annual for Boys*, not so much to mark his place, as for somewhere to keep the invitation. It stayed between a poem called 'The Fiddler of Dooney' and an account of how the natives of Borneo all lived together in what looked like long wooden attics. David wondered what it would be like if he and his Aunt Jean and Jacko all lived together in his attic, and if Jacko had gone off not to have all his hair cut off like Ritchie Dale and to stamp on concrete with his boots, but to be a head-hunter. The head-hunters of Borneo, and the wives and mothers and daughters of the head-hunters, didn't wear many clothes. David wondered if Jo-Jo the Dried-Up Man had been a head-hunter in real life. He certainly hadn't looked like anyone who lived in Viewforth Road, not even like Mr Elswick, who was possibly the most dried-up person that David knew. Jacko had obviously paid great attention to the head-hunters when the *King George V Empire Annual for Boys* had belonged to him, because these pages were greyer than the rest. It didn't seem likely anyway that the pages were well-thumbed because he had been turning to 'The Fiddler of Dooney'. David liked the poem, but he didn't understand any of it except the line about dancing like a wave of the sea. That seemed very off to him when he thought about the slow angular approach of the waves on the sand of the North Shore, and the way they unfurled along their length and broke irregularly. It would be a very strange sort of dance, like a sort of hovering or limping. David knew what dancing was really like. You held someone tightly and awkwardly, and slid and strode about trying not to look in the person's face. The music had to be quite quick on the whole, though it made people look very sad. David associated the Fiddler of Dooney with Mickey Rooney, whom he had seen in a film where he was a kind of musical magician bringing things to life. He could visualise his face presiding in goblin delight over some marching bananas. He was rather like Jacko, except that he wore a bow-tie and that his girl-friend, who wore a bow in her hair and a permanent expression of equal joy and wonder, seemed to adore him, and to be adored in return.

This adoration was puzzling. It only seemed to be acknowledged in films. In fact most films seemed to contain quite a lot of it. In real life it didn't work out like that. Mr Dale didn't adore Mrs Dale. Everyone said they used to hit each other. Mr Elswick didn't adore Mrs Elswick. They ignored each other. Dr Simpson didn't adore Mrs Simpson. They hardly ever seemed to be together. It was something younger people were supposed to do. Ritchie Dale was always with girls, but he didn't adore them. He supposed that Sylvia Elswick adored Jacko, but it made her very sad. Jacko didn't adore her. He seemed to be bored with her. But no one had ever paid her any attention before, and that seemed good enough for Sylvia. The only two people he knew who looked as though they got the sort of things out of adoration that you were supposed to: excited exchange of information, for example, long

conversations about planned fun, and a pleasure in touching each other, were Phyllis and his Aunt Jean. And that
couldn't count because they were both women. David
wondered if what he felt about Jill Simpson amounted to
adoration. It probably did, he thought, for he suddenly
felt quite grown up. It didn't even matter that Jill didn't
adore him. He had a vision of his own future that assured
him of the importance of his own experience. It was
nothing specific, no prophecy of events. Or at least not in
a positive sense: he somehow knew that he would not end
up with a job at Brickfields, married to Jill Simpson. It
was a more generalised intuition, a new awareness of
something he had no means of identifying. Some of it was
to do with having a future at all. Not all of it took place at
the same time. He had been running round the corner of
Viewforth Road, where the low red wall and trimmed
privet of the Boothroyds' garden were matched curve for
curve, conspiring to take the same direction, though in
colour, texture and origin so very different. There was
nothing particularly remarkable about this fact except that
David found himself remarking it. And consequent upon
that observation, mysteriously concurrent with it, came
the realisation that he too was there at the same time.
There he was, running past the corner at half past four on
a Thursday. Not only running past the corner, but knowing that he was running past the corner, and knowing that
he was knowing it. Other feelings like that occurred to
him on different occasions, but he knew they were all part
of the same thing. When the Japanese had attacked the
US Fleet at Pearl Harbor, Granny had just been calculating
how few shopping days there were left until Christmas.
They listened to the news in the lounge. For the first time
David understood that the war was not so much a state of
affairs that you lived with, like a family, but a series

of events, many of them unpredictable, many of them self-contradictory. And what was more, just as he had suddenly seen himself when running by the wall as being ascertainably 'there', observable to a hypothetical third party and yet himself in control of the force and effect of his appearances in the world, so he now saw that he had a relationship with the war as well. He had a relationship with everything. He was not only an onlooker. Pearl Harbor had occurred, and other events which had not yet occurred would undeniably do so. They were not part of some undifferentiated public spectacle, but real conditions of life that might have some effect on his own.

'That'll bring the Yanks into the war all right,' said Mr Elswick, with a gloomy satisfaction. 'They'll finish it off.' He was playing a low trump with an air of concealed cunning.

'Perhaps with the Yanks in the war they'll not be calling any more of our lads up,' said Jean.

'It's a bit late now,' said Granny.

'Aye,' said Mr Elswick darkly. 'What's gone is gone, and I dare say no regrets either.'

'What do you mean by that, Mr Elswick?' asked Jean.

But Mr Elswick refused to be drawn.

'It's not for me to say, is it?'

David knew from other conversations between Jean and Granny that it was to do with Jacko and Sylvia, but he did not know what it was about. Whenever he saw her, Sylvia looked even more subdued than usual. She always seemed to have a cold, dabbing at her nose with a dainty folded handkerchief like a dead rose.

Jean began to feel sorry for her.

'You know,' she said to Phyllis, 'they alway used to wallop her when she was little.'

'Yes, well, my mother was like that, too,' said Phyllis. 'She couldn't think of anything else.'

'No, I mean they used to wallop her all the time,' said Jean. 'That's why she looked so awful. That's why the boys used to chase her down the back. If you get walloped all the time then everyone else wants to wallop you, don't they? It shows. She's always snivelling.'

'Poor thing,' said Phyllis. 'She ought to have her adenoids out.'

'I'll bet you five pounds to a pinch of dog dirt they're not the only things she's going to want to have out,' said Jean.

'Jean,' exclaimed Phyllis. 'You don't mean . . .'

'Ssh,' said Jean, remembering David. They both looked under the table, where Captain Heart was conducting a daring rescue on a prisoner-of-war camp with hand grenades.

'Here,' said Jean. 'What are you doing with those matches? You'll set the carpet on fire.'

'He doesn't miss a thing, does he?' said Phyllis.

David wasn't sure whether he'd caught it or not. He knew it hadn't been thrown in his direction. Nothing ever was thrown in his direction, so he tended to give up trying to catch anything. He already knew very well from his own observation that whatever had been going on between Jacko and Sylvia wasn't going to finish just like that. Jacko's call-up wasn't a simple conclusion to the sort of thing that had been going on.

What had been going on?

Before his call-up the relationship had appeared to the general public, that is to say the concerned and the less-concerned inhabitants of Viewforth Road, to be an entirely conventional and somewhat half-hearted one of romantic assignations and neighbourly flirtation. David, and perhaps Jean, had had plenty of opportunity to witness the emotional undercurrents: the intensity of reproaches and earnestness of defensiveness that signalled a serious development in the relationship. David had seen more of it than his aunt, but had been much less certain of its interpretation. He had thought perhaps that Jacko was quite anxious to join up now that at last his papers had come. He could at least see that Sylvia wouldn't want him to. But then again, perhaps she might, so that she could admire him.

'My hero,' breathed Sylvia from the getaway jeep. She could never put down her buckets, and so could not take a direct part in the attack on the camp, but the buckets were useful for carrying grenades. Captain Heart and his faithful band of commandoes went in alone to rescue Jacko Turner, Ritchie Dale, Des Mullard and the other conscripts. They flipped the burning grenades over the parapet, and the German sentries fell from their towers with burning faces. Everyone, including the released prisoners, was covered in glory.

When Jacko came home on leave there was not yet much evidence of glory. His ears stuck out unnaturally from his head, and he was even more hungry than usual. What's more, instead of foraging for himself as he used to do, he was quite happy to sit in the kitchen with an air of lordly weariness and be served enormous platefuls. He reminded David of Robbo's father. Why did the army starve its soldiers? Perhaps they didn't have enough coupons in the army. And yet Jacko had to take his ration book with him.

Granny had to produce a second helping of fried bread, and to fill up the teapot. He appeared to have finished telling them about the army, because he started to tell them all over again from the beginning.

The next morning he gave them a demonstration of   89

squad drill in the back yard. Granny was impressed.

'Your father used to be able to do that,' she said.

Jacko was pleased, and showed them again. Jean sniffed, and went indoors.

'Isn't it bad for your boots?' she remarked as she went.

'It's smart,' sneered Jacko. 'It's *smart*, that's what it is!'

But she pretended not to hear him shouting after her. David had to clap extra loudly to keep up Jacko's self-esteem. In fact he clapped so loudly that Jacko went into the whole rigmarole for a third time. It was cold. Granny had to go and get on with the washing, but Jacko hardly noticed. He came in himself later, quite flushed with the effort.

Jean was darning his socks.

'I'm darning your socks,' she said. 'Have you been to see Sylvia?'

'You don't have to darn my socks,' said Jacko. He put his hands in his pockets and squared his shoulders. He said nothing about Sylvia.

Jean was silent for a while. Then she spoke again.

'I've never seen such big potatoes in a pair of socks in my life.'

'You don't have to darn my socks,' said Jacko again. 'We darn our own socks.'

'You could have fooled me,' said Jean. 'What did you bring them home for, then?'

Jacko waggled the handle of the warming oven at the bottom of the range with the toe of his boot. Then he took a deep breath, gave a short laugh, and left the kitchen.

It was the weekend of David's school 'play', which consisted of scenes from *Twelfth Night*, an adaptation of *A Christmas Carol* and songs from the junior forms. The headmistress had produced *Twelfth Night*. She insisted that all the male parts, even Fabian, Sir Andrew and the Clown, should wear beards because everyone in Elizabethan England wore a beard. The beards were all identical, woven with ginger wool on wire frames that hooked over the ears. There was an insufficient gap for the mouth, so that the beards became hot and wet. The actors were inaudible. It was like speaking through birds' nests.

By contrast, the story of Scrooge was a great success. It had been produced by Miss Mackie, and rehearsed with precision. She had so drilled the actors in the correct delivery of their lines that they all spoke with slight Scottish accents. Marley's Ghost was particularly effective, because he was played by a violent, tearful boy called Perkins of whom everyone in the school was afraid in any case because of his temper and his eczema. Tiny Tim was played by Jill. It seemed quite natural that Jill should have been chosen to act with this senior form. Although she looked very far from sickly, she was good at limping on her single crutch. When she spoke the last lines of the play in ringing tones ('God bless us, every one!') there was the slight ripple of a cheer amongst the audience, and Jill, as if extemporising an acknowledgment of this enthusiasm, though the action had been well rehearsed, stepped forward towards the audience and raised her green top hat. David wondered if the hat were really required for the part. It seemed a bit incongruous. But he felt obscurely excited and privileged to have seen her wearing it in a different context.

The songs came last. Sea shanties, Old Abram Brown, traditional airs and carols for the audience to sing. Miss Mackie conducted these from the piano, and it was at last David's turn to be on stage. At rehearsals he had learned how to sing with his hands clasped behind his back, and 91

he had attacked with great vigour the most vigorous of
the songs:

> 'Dashing away with the spoon in hand,
> Dashing away with the spoon in hand,
> Dashing away with the spoon in hand,
> She stole my heart away!'

He had been abashed when Miss Mackie had singled him
out and told him that those were not the right words. He
had thought they were, and they still seemed to him better
than the right words. He very much wanted to please Miss
Mackie, but something nearly always seemed to go wrong.
When he put a joke ink-blot made of black tin on her
register he thought it was a brilliant idea to turn an empty
ink-well on its side next to the blot, for greater realism.
But the ink-well had not been empty.

Jacko had not come to the school play, and there had
been a bit of an argument about it. He had gone to the
Savoy with Fred, and Harold Fletcher.

'I'd have thought you were sick of going out with men,'
said Jean. 'You do that all the time in the army. If you're
not going to come to hear David singing, why at least
don't you take Sylvia?'

'Listen, you,' said Jacko. 'Don't keep going on, will you?
Sylvia this, Sylvia that. You used to tell me off for seeing
her in the first place. I don't have to take Sylvia nowhere.'

'Oh no?' said Jean. 'You've led her right up the garden
path, haven't you? Don't you feel responsible?'

'Me?' asked Jacko. 'Responsible for what? I don't feel
responsible.'

This was a word which David had often heard Jean and
Granny use when talking about his father. He knew it was
a very serious word, to do with parents mostly, but quite
a bit to do with money. He knew that his father had sent

money, and he had had a letter, but Granny had told him that she didn't think he would come for Christmas, that he wouldn't be able to get away. David accepted that. His father was doing very important work in the war, much more important than Jacko for example, and it was quite understandable that (as David imagined) he would be brought his Christmas dinner in the cockpit of a Lancaster while he sorted out a bunch of coloured wires behind the controls. It might even be just a turkey sandwich and a mince pie, with perhaps a small Christmas cracker across the edge of the plate.

David didn't think his own Christmas holiday was at all jolly, come to think of it. There was a lot of whispering which he couldn't quite hear, and silences when he was in the room. The Elswicks came round even more than usual, with baleful faces, and then Mr Elswick turned up not with Mrs Elswick but with his sister, who was a very serious-looking woman, like a thin Mrs Thesiger. David was told to go and play in the attic.

He was disappointed by Jill's party, because he didn't know anyone except Jill and Phillie Lacey and they played games which he didn't understand. He felt very out of place. His aunt had said he had to wear his suit, and his shoes were well-polished. Everyone else was wearing quite scruffy clothes, and they ignored him. Where did they all come from, anyway, he wondered, since they weren't from school? The stars of the party were dark-haired twins in very short shorts and hand-knitted fishermen's jerseys. They had florid complexions and ran about a lot, winning all the prizes. David got the impression they were foreign. They were elaborately polite to Mrs Simpson, who hovered in the background with supplies of things to eat. The games were all organised by Robin Simpson, who at least seemed to enjoy them himself. Jill   93 hardly spoke to him at all, except in the last game they played, called 'Sardines', when all the lights were turned out and someone went off to hide. The point of the game was that if you found their hiding-place you yourself hid there with them, as quietly as possible, until someone else found you both and joined you, and so on. Jill insisted on being the person to hide, but no one could find her. David kept bumping into the other children in the dark, who would mutter crossly: 'Hasn't anyone found her *yet?*' and 'I don't think so.' It was David who found her first. Or rather, he wouldn't have found her if she hadn't hissed at him from the wardrobe in her parents' bedroom as he creaked by on the landing. 'I thought you said we weren't to come in here,' he said, as he crept in beside her among the high-heeled shoes. 'That's why no one will find us,' Jill mouthed in his ear. Then she held his neck, as though she were going to throttle him, and put her lips on his own, firmly and without movement. He felt her breath. She might have been blowing on him, or measuring for equality of features. Her face, because unseen, seemed the largest thing he had ever known in the world. And no one did find them.

Great Uncle Alfred and Aunt Bea came for Christmas dinner and everyone played Newmarket. In one hand Jacko got all the horses, but he was still under a cloud, and only Aunt Bea, who didn't know anything about it, was nice to him. David enjoyed playing with his presents, but secretly he had been hoping for some new Dinky toys and nobody had given him any. Jacko didn't give him anything at all. He had got some soap for Jean and Granny, which they had to share. They opened it together, one at each end like a cracker, and said they were very pleased with it. Even Jacko became embarrassed. He said he had had other presents for them, but had left them on the train. Great Uncle Alfred slept a lot, and then Christmas was over.

Soon after that Jacko went back to camp. He had to catch an early train, and so Granny had made sandwiches for him the night before. She got up herself, though. David heard their voices, when it was still dark. He tiptoed to the half-landing between the attic and the other bedrooms and stood by the grandfather clock, listening. But he still couldn't quite hear what they were saying: they had gone down to the kitchen. David didn't know whether he should go downstairs himself to say goodbye to Jacko. He knew that Granny, being Jacko's mother, had a special relationship with him but he did not quite know what it might be like now that Jacko was grown up. It couldn't be at all like his memory of his own mother, because he had been little then. It wasn't so long ago, but he had been much smaller. Much smaller, and very different. He stood on a chair and peered out of the attic window when he heard the front door slam, even though he knew that the only part of the street he would be able to see was the bit beyond Mrs Thesiger's towards the alley, not the direction that Jacko would take at all.

Afterwards the house seemed more empty of him than when he had originally left, which was strange because he'd been 'out' during his leave just as often as he used to be. That was when Jean started to be particularly nice to Sylvia, though it didn't seem to prevent Sylvia bursting into tears just as often.

When Jean took David to the pictures, Sylvia came as well. They went to the Laurel and Hardy at the Imperial, and sat in the ninepennies rather than the one-and-threes because Sylvia said she always sat in the ninepennies. Jean had a bag of mint imperials, which she and Phyllis were always sucking, and which David thought were appropriate to have at the Imperial. Sylvia said she preferred her liquorice allsorts, and David did too, because mint imperials were so hard to crunch and he was usually too impatient to suck them.

When the film was over and they were walking out, they saw that Phyllis had been at the film too, sitting behind them all the time in the one-and-threes. She was with another nurse and both were still in uniform. They were accompanying two servicemen in hospital blues, one with his tunic loose over one arm in a sling, the other, as David immediately saw in a lurch of disturbance and fascination, with something very wrong with his face.

Jean naturally went up to talk to them in the foyer. She was surprised to see Phyllis in town, because it wasn't the weekend, but of course she would still be on duty. Getting the boys back on their feet, getting them out and about, showing themselves in public, was part of what the rehabilitation was all about. Some of the nurses didn't like doing it, but Phyllis never minded. She had told Jean that it was a way of getting out herself, otherwise she'd feel quite cooped up all the week at Seaton Hall. Some of them she could take home to see her mother, who didn't mind making tea for them. It was harder to do that with the bad ones, but they were the ones that needed it most. Like 'Burroughs'. Phyllis had spoken about 'Burroughs' before, and Jean was curious to see him, even if she was a bit scared.

Sylvia was terrified. She hung back, pretending to look at the stills of the film that was coming next week. She hunted in her crumpled paper bag for the last liquorice allsort to give to David. She even kept David with her by kneeling down on the maroon-and-gold hemispheres of the cinema carpet to tie up his shoelace. David didn't think his shoelace had been undone, but he went along with

96

the charade because he didn't particularly want to go too near himself. And yet he did want to look.

He thought his aunt was extraordinary. She had marched right up to them and was talking away as though she had just met Phyllis at the front door and they were alone. She didn't seem at all nervous. And yet she was like an actress who has made her entrance on a stage. All the audience drifting past them stared at her and at the nurses and the servicemen as though they were famous. They were shaking hands even, which was something that David knew from films people did when they met for the first time but which he couldn't remember seeing anyone do in real life. The man with his arm in the sling was looking at her all the time, his chin slightly lowered, his eyes alert and a smile on his face that seemed to be agreeing with whatever his aunt was saying.

The other man was short, but stood very erect, and just a little further back from the group than the others. Part of his face was hidden by what looked to David like cotton-wool, and he also wore what was obviously a coarse wig. What could be seen of his face was unnaturally red and shiny. There was an eye, but it didn't seem to be looking out of his face in quite the right place, and sometimes it seemed to be shut for much longer than it would take to blink. David thought he might be wearing a mask.

Suddenly, unbelievably, he was being made to say hello to the men. He blushed, and at first held out the wrong hand to be shaken. The man with the sling laughed. Phyllis asked him how he had liked the film.

He felt as he had felt when he marched up on to the stage with the others to sing 'Dashing away with the spoon in hand' in front of the bright lights and the dark sea of faces beneath it. But he was alone this time. Sylvia seemed to have bolted.

Phyllis introduced the man with the sling as Flying Officer Kent, and the man with the face as Pilot Officer Burroughs.

'It's too complicated to explain,' she said, 'but we all know that's not his name. It was a mistake. But it sort of stuck, and we all call him that.'

Very slowly Pilot Officer Burroughs spoke. The mouth worked behind the seamed face, elusive words struggling against its immobility. David thought it must be like answering the dentist's questions when all his equipment is hooked over your teeth. You are anxious to tell him how it feels, but don't believe that he can understand you.

David wanted to say that he didn't understand, to save him all this wasted effort. Everyone seemed to have stopped. Phyllis's animation was suspended on a surprised smile. The other nurse was looking at him.

David realised that Pilot Officer Burroughs had at last finished, and that he had even belatedly understood one of his words, which had at first sounded like 'gated'. He also realised, when Jean nudged him, that he was being personally addressed. That some reply to what the man had said was expected.

He felt tormented. It was not so much his inability to reply, as the extraordinary effort the man had made to speak to him that obsessed him. What could it be that was worth the strain of that hideous ventriloquism?

His aunt was looking brightly at him with that expression he well recognised in grown-ups, compounded of pride, encouragement and irritation. He knew he was letting her down. Minutes seemed to go by. He went alternately cold and hot.

He did not know whether to look at the face or not. If he looked at it the man would think he was staring. If he didn't look at it, the man would think he was frightened. He supposed that he was frightened.

Then suddenly he understood what the man had said. It was obvious. He was asking him if he had enjoyed the film.

'Oh, yes,' said David gratefully. 'It was grand.'

There was no ascertainable expression on Pilot Officer Burrough's face, but the glistening slit of the mouth seemed to tighten. His hand came up to touch David's elbow slightly. Then he half turned away.

Everybody else seemed to start speaking at once. Jean made loud goodbyes, saying that she must go and find Sylvia, laughing and apologising for her. Flying Officer Kent looked rueful.

'Another fine mess you've got her into,' he said.

Everybody laughed again, but without acknowledging the implications of the joke. Phyllis gave David a kiss, and said she would see him soon. They all began to move out of the foyer and into the street. Their breath made disappearing fumes in the night air.

They found Sylvia outside and went their ways.

10

He knew now that his name was really Hamilton. This was what he had been told. The doctors would use that name, or more often than not his first name, Freddy. He knew that he came from New Zealand, and that was why he hadn't been visited. It was too far. But for him it was too far in time as well as space. He could summon up no images of his life before the war. It was as though the crash had completed a process of withdrawal already begun, as though simply to become a pilot, with the pilot's vows of sacrifice and acceptance of risk, was to become free of family ties, and as though to become faceless was the flourish of the signature of sacrifice on his contract, after which it was impossible ever to return.

Whatever life he had once had as Freddy Hamilton was now quite defaced. He more readily accepted his limbo existence as Burroughs. Burroughs was like a role he played. It was like treading a stage and hearing applause. On the lips of the nurses the name represented a category of their duty, its tone compounded of awe, protective mockery, and tenderness.

'There we are then!' was the cheerful claim to have fulfilled the simplest of these duties. He could gauge his acceptability as a human being by the quality of these exclamations, and the briskness of the nurses' appearances. Dressed, and bandaged, he was presentable. He could be accompanied, taken on walks, even to the cinema. In the ward, in the aftermath of an operation, his inability to function was a reminder of how close a damaged body was to the inhuman. His facelessness created fear.

He could use their own faces as mirrors, in fact. He began to train himself in noticing their expressions. The busy averted preoccupation with chart or thermometer, the brave glance, the steeled question, the involuntary amused look: he knew there were bad days and good days.

Real mirrors he banished like the wicked queen in fairy tales. They were like unbelievable windows into disaster or the future, walls grown cruel, sprung traps. But in the end you could not avoid the merciless intelligence of the mirror. It was the most characteristically human of all inventions, and the most radical. It was closer to laughter or tears than to the wheel. It seemed indeed to be not a technological invention at all, but a psychological one.

He could not remember looking in a window and thinking: 'Freddy'. He could not remember looking in a mirror and seeing his own face. He had received a letter from his mother which meant nothing to him. That was like looking in a mirror and seeing a different face.

Everything became a mirror: faces, letters, the cinema screen. Hardy in patient exasperation wiping a line of custard from his eyebrow, fastidiously, yet leaving the rest of his face plastered. Hardy thus disfigured, in collusion with the audience in his weary criticism of Laurel's mishap that had so smothered him, looking at the audience in resignation.

The audience had laughed.

Hardy's defacement was a rebuke to his natural charm and dignity. That charm was so often ingratiating and opportunist, that its deflation was satisfying. His face was put out.

And yet it was Laurel who was upset. It was Laurel who did not know which way to turn.

The audience laughed all the more.

That little boy with Phyllis's friend, was it her brother? Her nephew? He had looked to each side of himself, as if for help that he knew could not possibly be forthcoming, as he had struggled with the embarrassment of not quite hearing what had been said to him.

What was the boy's name? David?

It had seemed important to gain David's interest and respect, however slight, however socially dutiful. And his perfectly ordinary, socially dutiful question must have seemed like a rebuke, simply because he could not speak properly. It must have seemed like a challenge to be understood, which the right sort of sympathy might have cheerfully met. It was as though not understanding was a failure of charity. And that spurious guilt had descended on the boy as completely and suddenly as Laurel's crying face replaced his simpleton face.

He had been aghast at creating such misery, however momentary. The boy's face had become, as they all stood around lamely rooted in the cinema foyer, a flushed and staring simulacrum of his own, another mirror.

He had been in danger of becoming a film himself. A young director who had been in the GPO Film Unit, probably finding gnarled trawlermen for John Grierson, was compiling a documentary about military heroism. Oh, he was very good at locating heroes: his sympathetic interest was like a paraded medal, symbol of an energy beyond the call of duty. It brought an instantaneous response. Everyone wanted to help, except possibly the heroes. There was to be music by a composer who could produce abundant chords of Elgarian majesty just sufficiently bolstered with wrong notes to emphasise the futility of what was displayed on the screen.

He did not want to become this film, and tried to tell Dr Simpson so without seeming ungracious. He was after all by now the longest-serving patient at Seaton Hall, and if he had no existence as Freddy he did perhaps have one as Burroughs. As Burroughs he was not only the object of the nurses' attention, but also a prize exhibit, a triumph of medical engineering. He did not want to let them all down. Sir James had already been filmed, seated impressively behind a desk, like the Prime Minister on newsreels. But that was all very well. He belonged there as much as he belonged in the operating theatre. It was even a kind of alternative theatre, where he played the role of explanatory chorus to the high drama of the knife. The desk required his reassuring head and shoulders and clasped hands as it required the untouched blotter, the twin inkwells and the small silver vase with the single bowed rose. But they could not film Freddy at the controls, which was where he belonged: why should they film instead the hapless and displaced Burroughs?

Somehow his predicament was never resolved, and no decision actually taken. The film director and his team were allowed to turn up at the New Year Dance, men wearing incongruously informal clothes, baggy flannels and tight fairisle pullovers. The camera was erected stiffly in one corner of the hall, free to gaze on the proceedings with all the spurious participation and unconnecting friendliness of a blind man, its black twin spools as blank as a pair of dark glasses. They pretended to film nothing in particular, but whenever he moved he felt himself to 103 be the object of that mechanical attention. It was as though he were a tethered animal.

There were streamers and paper hats, iced cakes and lemonade. It was more like a children's party than a dance. And Phyllis looked after him like a child, helped him even though he no longer wanted to be helped, and refused to dance with anyone. Would she have danced with him if he had asked her? He did not ask her. He could not have danced, for he could barely see when he moved about, and was sometimes dizzy when he simply stood. Besides, he basked in his knowledge of the more intimate contact of therapy, with its close support and clutches, its staggering and unbalanced hugs. What was the stiffness of a tango to the months of blind perambulation in Phyllis's arms?

The couples stalked and pivoted across the parquet to the strains of an ad hoc band that was all percussion. It was like dancing to a public-address stethoscope. Phyllis's friend Jean, the girl he had met at the cinema, was dancing with Flying Officer Kent. Kent had his good hand splayed against her back; the other was in its sling, half-hidden by the loose tunic. The attitude looked deliberate, aloof, even raffish. As they turned, his gaze went just ahead of their movement, scanning the room as if to notice some insult.

The girl had a good figure. She was flushed and bright-eyed, with a contained smile above her sturdy little jaw, and a thatch of curls. She held Kent up at arms' length appraisingly, as if he were a suit of clothes she was about to put on. He felt that Phyllis was watching them all the time, even while she was looking after him, making sure that he had a drink and at the same time knowing whereabouts in the room the pair were, like a mother at a picnic. She was like a mother who knows just how far her baby can crawl before she becomes anxious; brisk and bright and unrelaxed. A baby aunt. He wished Phyllis's friend had brought the boy. He could have tried to talk to the boy in ways that he could not talk to the nurses or to the other patients. But Seaton Hall was not a place for children. In fact the whole occasion was a grotesque mockery of the rituals of courtship, for it did not seem likely that many of the men who were not fathers already could very soon become so. And the nurses danced with them as dutifully as with their own fathers. Some of them even danced with each other, for many of the damaged servicemen were content to sit against the walls, as cumbersome in their bandages as in fancy dress which they dare not risk on the dance floor for fear of losing the chance of a prize. And there were no real prizes, for a nurse (like the professional status she aspires to) was a surrogate sister, not to be wooed.

He wondered what would happen if he were to slip his hand behind the starched apron-front of Phyllis's uniform to find the two crucial buttons that would allow his crawling fingers entrance to assess the weight of the hoarded treasure that filled and stretched it. He imagined the uniform pulled away or slipped off, his hands undoing further buttons and clasps, rolling down elastic. He hardly knew whether to be surprised or not at the indifference he felt at such thoughts, nor if he should challenge his indifference further. He risked a rapid projection of outrageous images, as promising but temporarily unverifiable as a cinema trailer, in which he was quite alone and intimate with the baby aunt. His imagination allowed her all eagerness, compliance and invention, but his senses were unstirred.

He had been over all this before, many times, staring half-blind in the lavatory at his limp sinker as a princess might stare at an unredeemed frog, in a torment of futile hope.

On the dais Sir James was making a speech. The camera had been repositioned with some fuss and deliberation, and Sir James, exposed to its unstinting reflection of his photogenic status, orated to it as if the medical achievements of the Unit required special justification in its presence. He spoke of faith, of devotion, of miracles, but he spoke in the manner of a company chairman hoping to be returned to Parliament, one thumb appearing to search restlessly in a waistcoat pocket for a non-existent cough lozenge. Then Sister spoke, and one of the nurses brought her chrysanthemums.

There was applause, as though the year's work at Seaton Hall had been a dramatic performance, and a little naval rating called Sparrow, who had been injured in a boiler-room explosion, stood up to speak for the patients. In the course of his speech, which contained many jokes, he slowly and elaborately lit and smoked a cigarette with his one hand, the thumb of which was in fact his big toe, grafted by Sir James in yet another of his bizarre pioneering operations. To a man who had once sunk a ten-yard putt with the handle of a mashie all things were possible. Sir James bowed in response, glowering benignly with a mixture of Promethean distance and canny bonhomie, and shortly afterwards midnight struck.

The New Year brought no real hopes. The film was a mistake. Drifting into its making without ever giving his assent, submitting himself to close-ups, he knew that it could never be shown. He was too hideous.

11

When David went back to school he found that he was in a new form. So was Phillie Lacey, and another boy called Ronald Brock. He felt strange without his friends, who made scornful jokes about it but at the same time seemed to be in awe of him. When he went to speak to Jill Simpson in the playground, she wouldn't talk to him. Robbo kept his distance as well. There was a new craze for collecting cigarette packets, with Robbo becoming the prime source of stock and arbiter of relative values. David had no immediate access to cigarette packets now that Jacko had gone, but Jean asked Phyllis if she could collect them at Seaton Hall. Nothing was easier, and there proved to be lots of exotic brands from foreign servicemen being treated there. After the half-term break David's collection quite clearly put Robbo's in the shade. Robbo didn't like that a bit.

One day when David was showing a notably rare specimen, a 50 tin of Player's cork-tipped Mild, Robbo came over to inspect it, opening the lid too far so that it bent.

'You did that on purpose,' said David. 'Look, it doesn't fit now.'

'Give it here, then,' said Robbo, bending it back again.   107

'Don't!' said David. 'You've gone and made it worse!'

Robbo just laughed, but some of the others thought he'd gone too far. The lid had come half away from the bottom. Robbo didn't even pretend to try to fit it back again. He joggled the tin roughly, and then held up the parts in each hand.

'It's not very well made,' he said.

'You!' shouted David in a fury, leaping at him. But Robbo did not flinch. He put out his fist, and David felt the whole front of his face burst, nose, lips and teeth. It felt as though his mouth had come apart, and he daren't touch it. Everyone looked at him aghast, and then at Robbo.

'I didn't do it,' said Robbo, looking round. 'He did it. You all saw him attack me.'

There was a salty taste in David's mouth. Miss Mackie took him away to sponge it.

'Poor wee mouth,' she said as she dabbed gently at it. David winced. Then Miss Mackie kissed the top of his head and Robbo got into a lot of trouble.

When David looked in the mirror that evening his lips were red and swollen, bright and shining like the parts of that pilot's face that he'd been able to see. His aunt had said the pilot had been burnt, but he couldn't understand why that made him look sticky. Things that were burnt looked black usually. His own lips looked a bit like Sylvia Elswick's lips used to look after spending an evening with Jacko in the lounge. But they hurt! Did Sylvia's hurt? Did kissing hurt? He knew that having babies hurt. Perhaps everything that men and women did together in private hurt. In that case, why did they do it? He tried to imagine how much the pilot's face had hurt. Was it like this, only all over? No, it must have been worse, much worse. How much worse? Phyllis had said that they'd had to piece his face together again from other bits of him, even from bits of his bottom. David couldn't help laughing at the thought, and then wished he hadn't: his lip had split again.

He took it to his aunt.

'You're coming apart, you are,' she said, dabbing at it.

'Ow!' groaned David, squirming away. 'What are you doing?'

'Keep still,' said Jean. 'I'm putting antiseptic on.'

'I've had all that,' protested David.

'Well, you're having it again.'

David compared her attentions to those of Miss Mackie. His aunt was slower, and softer. He held on to her neck, and investigated the sprung trap of a curl, letting it open and then roll shut at the movement of his finger.

She smiled at him.

'Always in the wars,' she said.

'Perhaps I'll be in *the* war,' he replied.

'I hope not,' she said. 'I hope you stay just where you are. We don't want anything happening to you.'

David wondered what was happening to those who *had* gone off to the war. They didn't seem to get very far, Jacko somewhere in Wiltshire, Ritchie Dale in Scotland, his father in a hangar making miniature daggers, but it was far enough. The lads at Seaton Hall belonged somewhere else, too. Where was the war itself, though? Hitler had given up on Britain. We'd had our battle, and now we were just carrying on, patching ourselves up, and preparing to fight back.

He thought of Jacko preparing to fight, stamping his drill like a carthorse on the parade ground, firing guns. He'd be useless! Jacko couldn't put his mind to one thing for a minute at a time. And he was a coward, too. Even Granny had said so, and she must be the one who loved him most. But David knew that when Granny said he   109 was a coward she wasn't thinking about the war. It was something to do with Sylvia Elswick.

Sylvia hadn't come round to the house since Christmas. Mr Elswick's sister had been once, but David had been sent upstairs so he still didn't know what she had to say to them. He looked down at her from the top of the stairs when she left, but she didn't see him. Her coat seemed to have even more silk loops and buttons than Granny's. She did them all up silently, facing away from Granny, who was standing in the doorway of the front room looking at her. She let herself out.

David knew that Jacko was under a cloud, and when Mrs Thesiger asked after him one day when he met her coming home from school, the way she did so made him feel that she must know it, too. It was as though there was something to be ashamed of. Perhaps the whole street knew what it was, and he didn't.

Then suddenly he knew, and once he knew he realised that he had known it all the time. Jacko was coming home again on special leave to be married to Sylvia Elswick.

'Better late than never,' said Mr Elswick. 'Better wait than sever.' Jean had rolled her eyes at this, and Granny had cried into her handkerchief, but David knew that really they were all very excited.

He had never seen anyone married before, and wasn't quite sure after it was over that anything very much had happened. Everyone dressed up not only in their best clothes but in clothes that he had never seen before. His aunt Jean wore a hat with a veil. Mr Elswick wore a bowler. Uncle Alfred and Aunt Bea were monumental, in black as if for a funeral. David thought they looked grander than the Mayor and Lady Mayoress when they'd come to his school for the Harvest Festival. Granny wore furs even

110   bigger than Mrs Thesiger's, and Sylvia had a new costume

which her mother kept saying she should have let out. Jacko wore his uniform, but even that seemed different from the last time David had seen it. Apart from the clothes, and being photographed in them on the chilly steps of the register office, the only other special thing was everyone fitting in at Number 20 for a chicken dinner, and that wasn't very different from Christmas except that they didn't play games. David had even suggested that they did play games.

'Games?' said Mr Elswick, with a laugh. 'There's been enough games already, lad.'

Jacko wondered why they hadn't had a reception at the Savoy, but everyone pretended not to hear him.

After dinner Mrs Elswick cried, and then went up the street with Mr Elswick, who forgot his bowler hat and had to come back for it. Sylvia and Jacko slept together in Jean's room because it was bigger, and Jean had moved to Jacko's room. David thought that was very unfair on his aunt, and offered her the attic. She didn't want the attic. Stirring a cup of cocoa, she said she'd half a mind to go and live with Phyllis. Then Granny began to cry.

'How can you live with Phyllis?' she said eventually. 'Phyllis has to live at Seaton Hall. She's a nurse.'

'Well, I could be a nurse, too,' said Jean, throwing the spoon in the sink.

'It's all them pilots gone to your head,' said Granny.

'It's not her head they're going to,' said Jacko, coming into the kitchen.

'Get out, you!' stormed Jean. She looked around for something to throw at him. He sniggered and left before she could find anything. He had wanted a glass of water, and David was reminded of the night when he had come down in search of one himself and heard Jacko and Sylvia in the lounge.

'You're a one to talk, you are!' Jean shouted after him.

But Jacko wasn't really any longer anyone to talk. It was a solitary remark, the very last of the old Jacko. He went upstairs with his glass of water, and at the end of the week went back to the barracks, a subdued and married man. Sylvia didn't go home then, as David had presumed she would. She stayed on in Jean's room, very often till nine o'clock in the morning, shuffling around the kitchen in her dressing gown.

'Don't you mind?' David asked his aunt.

Jean just shrugged.

David minded. He minded for Jean's sake, but he also minded because it was the room, the very bed even, where he had slept with Jean when he first came to Viewforth Road. The fact that Jean could move out of it so easily, could even suggest, however lightly, moving out of the house, disturbed the centre of his universe. Would she really want to go and look after the servicemen at Seaton Hall as Phyllis did? David could tell the difference between Phyllis and Jean: Phyllis was sturdy, patient, unmovable; Jean liked to be pleased, was restless for something. He didn't know what it was, but he knew that she would change if she found it. He didn't want her to change. He didn't want her to go away. He didn't want her to move out of her room, even.

But though he minded Sylvia being in Jean's room, he didn't really mind Sylvia. He would be about to go to school, and she would wander in her nightdress into the kitchen and make herself some All-Bran and warm milk. Nobody else ever had warm milk with their cereal. David would be late for school because he liked to stay and watch Sylvia having her breakfast. Jean would have gone to work long ago, and Granny was busy doing the things that Granny always did, but Sylvia took all the time in the world and David was fascinated. She ate her cereal in tiny mouthfuls with her mouth open, looking out of the window. She never made toast, perhaps because that would have meant getting up from the table, and she never used a plate: she would balance the pieces of her bread and marmalade on top of the knife laid across her empty cereal bowl. Very occasionally she might come out of her trance, and look at David as though she had never seen him before. Then she would look down at her bread and marmalade and take another little bite.

It was as though they had acquired a pet animal. Everyone felt fond and protective, but she was a slight nuisance. There seemed no question of her taking David on an outing to Bellside Landing. Although of everyone he knew she had the right combination of time, authority and resources, she seemed since her marriage to Jacko to have yielded all of these, slight as in fact they may have been, to some higher power. She seemed quite content to do nothing. She basked in her animal existence as fully as if she knew that nobody could take it away from her.

And indeed nobody could take it away. When she started knitting little square pieces of ribbed white wool, Granny told David that she was going to have a baby.

David thought this must be the most important secret of all, much more important than their wedding. As soon as he heard, he went straight back into the front room where Sylvia was sitting in front of the fire to give her a kiss. And because it was an important kiss he kissed her directly on the lips, those little pinched-up lips that always gave the impression that she was slightly nauseated. Even as he did it, David wasn't quite sure that it was the right thing to do. He felt the kiss should last longer than the conventional peck of greeting, so he held his lips there 113 while steadying himself with each hand on an arm of the chair she was sitting in. Her eyes opened wider in surprise, and her lips opened too, as if involuntarily. She was eating a liquorice allsort and David could taste the sweet tarry fragrance of the liquorice in her wet mouth. He pressed his lips with all the formal fervour of congratulation, but hers responded beyond any social code, like something out of nature. It was like a glistening snail coming out of its shell and putting out horns. The kiss seemed to travel right down the sides of David's body to the tops of his legs. Then suddenly the liquorice allsort was inside his own mouth. Sylvia giggled.

'When will the baby come?' he asked, to cover his embarrassment. He hadn't known what to do with the sweet. He couldn't spit it out. Perhaps he should have pushed it back with his tongue, like a game. But it was too late. He swallowed it.

He hadn't imagined that a kiss could be like that. It was so different from the hard fierce little slit of Jill's mouth. He must have been blushing.

'It'll be a little spring baby,' she said, smoothing down the piece of her knitting. 'It'll be delivered in the hospital.'

David thought she spoke of it like a chicken, as though she'd ordered it, particularly not a big one, but too big for the postman to get it through the letter-box. He knew all about babies, though, because Robbo had told him in great detail, and Mr Blencowe had done some drawings on the blackboard. He'd never really thought the process through in terms of real people. It must be a bit like posting a letter, in fact, or putting a sweet in someone's mouth.

'Would you like another liquorice allsort?' asked Sylvia.

'No thanks,' said David.

She was holding the pieces of her knitting together,

pinching them where the seams would be. They didn't look like real clothes. They looked more like something you might make for Christmas that wasn't useful, like a tea-cosy or a bag for clothes pegs.

Was Jacko responsible for all this? Far from taking command of such an adventure, he seemed to have been demoralised and demoted, seeking his military exile gratefully. He seemed to have left Sylvia behind him at Number 20 like a bookmark or a piece in a board game. She represented an episode in his life which was now suspended. She sat by the fire waiting for a six to be thrown, but Jacko had lost interest in the game.

When David tried to talk to Jean about it, she didn't seem to care.

'Don't they want her at home any more?' he said.

'They think Jacko should look after her now,' she replied.

'Why?'

'That's what husbands do.'

'Jacko doesn't seem much like a husband to me. He isn't even here.' David pondered for a while, and then he added: 'I expect Mrs Elswick doesn't want them because the baby will cry all the time.'

Jean lifted her shoulders in helpless agreement. She hadn't been quite the same since that night after Christmas when they'd been to see the Laurel and Hardy at the Imperial. She'd been to the pictures again several times with Roger Kent. The last time, he'd called at the house and spoken to David who was sitting in the kitchen with his books.

'What's this, then?' he had asked, his gaze, at once furtive and inquisitive, sweeping the room.

David didn't like Flying Officer Kent, who didn't say very much, but was watchful and critical.

115

'My homework,' said David.

'Oh, we're doing homework now, are we?' said Flying Officer Kent. 'Jolly good.'

When Jean appeared, with more face-powder on than David had ever seen before, Kent put his good arm round her, sideways, like someone about to have his photograph taken. The next time David saw him, his other arm was out of its sling and he could wiggle one of its fingers. Not long after that he was gone for good.

'Well, what did you think would happen, Jean?' said Phyllis, commiserating.

'I don't know what I thought,' Jean replied.

'There's a war on,' said Phyllis, uselessly.

'No need to tell me that,' said Jean. 'Even Sid Molyneux's got his papers.'

'Crikey, they're really scraping the barrel now.'

Even Jean had to laugh, though she still had her handkerchief out.

David hated Flying Officer Kent, and he hated Sid Molyneux. He even had mixed feelings about Jacko. Why did men always have to make women cry? He took every opportunity to listen to Jean and Phyllis talking about these hard cases. It was much like listening to the radio, except that instead of going into the lounge and switching it on, he had to hide in one of his hiding-places and wait for Jean and Phyllis to make their tea. The boiling kettle always unlocked confessions and confidences, and they less often took their tea upstairs now that Sylvia had taken over Jean's bedroom.

'You're not still thinking about Roger Kent, are you, Jean?'

'Oh, not really.'

'You are, you know. I don't think he was worth it, myself.'

'He was lovely, Phyllis. He took me for dinner at the Castle Hotel.'

'Yes, you told me. I don't think it's that much better than the Savoy.'

'That's not the point.'

'The point is, Jean, that he hasn't written to you, and he's not going to write. You'd have been better off with Burroughs. Don't look so shocked. What is it? Don't look like that! He's a fine boy, is Freddy.'

Jean shuddered.

'Oh Phyllis, I couldn't go near him. I couldn't. I don't know how you manage it, I really don't. You're not telling me he's still there, after all this time?'

'He's not at all well, Jean. He's had twenty-seven operations, but some of the grafts don't take. The blood haemoglobin is too low, and there's no proper circulation.'

'I just couldn't even look at him.'

'It's funny. You get used to it. He's very brave. You can't imagine what it was like for him coming into town that time, or going to the dance. Putting on that dreadful wig.'

'I'm sorry, Phyllis, it's just me, I know. Is it worse behind the bandages?'

There was no reply to this. David was keeping very still, to catch everything that might be said. But there didn't seem to be much to be said. After a while, Phyllis went on:

'Sometimes he just wants to cry, but his face won't cry. It sort of gasps. I have to hold him. He just turns to me, gasping. It'd do him good to cry properly. He needs a good cry, like a baby.'

It sounded as though Phyllis was almost crying herself. David thought it was a different sort of crying from Jean's or Sylvia's. She wasn't crying for herself, but for someone   117 else. Sylvia didn't cry so much now anyway. She seemed to be quite content, sitting there with her stomach covered with her knitting like a ploughed hillside under snow. Her baby would do all her crying for her. And then Jean would have somebody else to look after. Why, by the time it came along David would be much older, quite able to take care of himself. And by the time it was David's age, David would be even older than his aunt and might be a Wing Commander.

David knew that he couldn't predict the future, not even over the short span that immediately concerned him. He did not know, for example, that he was to see the burnt pilot again, and that he was to get in the end to Bellside Landing.

It came about because of a reconciliation with Jill, who had also been moved up to David's new form at half-term, apparently because Dr Simpson and his wife had turned up at the school to tell the headmistress that she shouldn't be left behind. David could believe it, because he knew that Jill's father was held in great respect. And he knew that Jill was used to getting her way in everything. Was that why she had been so stand-offish? Because she hadn't been moved up?

For a time, then, they were friends again. But not the same kind of friends as she was with Phillie Lacey and a new but older girl called Marjorie Miller. Marjorie Miller had a very accusing personal sort of smile, as though she had noticed something disgraceful about you and wanted to get you worried about it. The three of them always had secrets. But they respected David.

It wasn't quite the same as with Robbo, though. He could never say things like 'Let's go to Mrs Tewkins!' quite as casually, because he was afraid of rebuff. Pleasures needed to be more calculated, somehow. It wasn't clear who decided on the trip to Bellside Landing. Perhaps it was Jill, because in the end it turned out that they needn't work out how to get there by bus as her father would take them in his car. But it was David who really wanted to go, and therefore the command of the expedition was instinctively felt to be his.

'We could catch a boat and go off anywhere!'

Although offered as an Easter treat, it seemed also to be part of Dr Simpson's work. He proposed to leave them at Bellside Landing with a picnic while he drove back to the bridge at Eelstock and went out to Seaton Hall. They were to take the Bellside Ferry across the Hebble and join him there at tea-time. To David all these precise geographical arrangements were puzzling, exciting, unclear. Instead of driving north they drove inland, through the farming valleys. Eelstock was a sprawling conglomeration of old fishing wharves, with the Fixby cannery on one side of the estuary and rows of warehouses on the other. David had imagined that they would be driving further and further from human habitation to a world of sand and sky and wading birds. In fact, Bellside Landing was a small resort with a marine pool, a putting-green and an enormous barren flagstaff. The wind seemed to come at them from all directions, ruffling Phillie's hair so that pink scalp showed beneath her punished red curls and lifting Jill's plait stiffly out behind her navy-blue raincoat like the tiller of a boat. Marjorie wore a woolly hat.

'Rather you than me,' said Dr Simpson, as he left them there. 'Four o'clock sharp.'

Jill had a watch, a big red one on which Mickey Mouse wagged the seconds with one finger, like a jitterbug. They ate their picnic almost immediately, as much out of curiosity as hunger. They saved their lemonade money for ice-creams and drank from a green cast-iron fountain 119

JOHN FULLER

which had gold-faced lions for legs and a pudgy gold boy
on top. There was no one about, and nothing much to do.
Even the ice-creams were disappointingly watery. David
felt responsible for everything but had no information and
no suggestions. They looked at comic postcards outside a
shop, and then took the ferry across the little estuary.
Above the chugging of the engine they could hear the
mournful cries of gulls, apparently tormented by any
movement that was not theirs.

Once on the old wooden jetty on the other side, David
felt that perhaps their adventure might begin. Avoiding
the single track road that led ultimately back to the
wharves, they investigated the sands around the promontory. It was so flat and wild that the true southward
direction was not at first apparent. They were tempted
to walk out towards the channel for fishing boats that
meandered like a ribbon through the sand, but soon found
that it was too wet. They tied their shoes round their necks
and waded across the hidden ribbed valleys and pools, far
from the shore. As they turned away, moving as he had
always known they must, directly southwards instead of
north, David was seized by a sadness quite beyond any
immediate disappointment. He was used to disappoint-
ments anyway, and had begun to learn that even if what
you expect to happen doesn't happen then something else
usually does which may be a compensation just because
it is unexpected. It could be something quite small, like
looking forward to Mrs Tewkins and getting no answer at
her front door, but then finding that there were ground
rice moulds with golden syrup for tea. Or it could be
something like the mermaid, which wasn't at all what he
had hoped for, but had provided instead Jo-Jo the Dried-
Up Man and the Largest Maggot in the World. Jill's party
had been disappointing, but he remembered her sudden

120

direct grip in the wardrobe, the dry lips crushed against his and the smell of soap, dust and leather.

His sadness now was nothing like that. He was glad to have known what Bellside Landing was like. He liked the feel of the gritty sand between his toes, even though his feet were icy. He had saved a ginger biscuit from the picnic, and though it had broken in half it was carefully wrapped in a paper bag in his trouser pocket and he could feel it against his leg as he walked. He was perfectly happy to be with Jill, Phillie and Marjorie, who were as varied a threesome as could be imagined: Marjorie tall, dark, sharp-nosed; Jill medium-sized, blonde, snub-nosed; Phillie small, red-haired, and freckles. He didn't mind if they walked on ahead and didn't take much notice of him. But he was sad, and he couldn't have explained it.

Perhaps it was something to do with Seaton Hall, which eventually came into view ahead of them beyond the dunes. They played silly games of pursuit along the rabbit paths, keeping hidden behind tussocks, extemporising more and more complicated rules of allegiance. Although the crests of the dunes, with their scooped craters and turfy runnels, were the most exciting part, it was easy to be caught. There were lower slopes where you could properly hide, but the sand was less fine and dry. Sometimes on the lower hollows and knolls a damp and splintered plank protruded from the sand, like the vanilla pod that Granny kept in the jar of caster sugar in the larder. Below that was gritty sand, a scum line of stinking seaweed, tarry stones, bleached rope-ends. It was a margin of drift and wreckage, where sea and wind reasserted their slow power to destroy. And as they moved in their game closer and closer to Seaton Hall, David felt that they were approaching a similar tideline of human abandonment: the half-used golf course, the outer greens ragged and

121

flagless; collapsed fencing; the beginning of a road half-drifted over; a deserted concrete pill-box. It was as though a town crumbled at its edges. It was like being drawn back into a frozen whirlpool.

And there on the perimeter was Seaton Hall, grey turrets facing the sea. It might have been a railway station without a line, a beached battleship, an ogre's castle. Its enchanted inhabitants seemed to have stumbled out of doors as if into a light they could not yet face. They sat on benches in the April sun with heads bowed, faces averted from its healing powers.

Some of the others stood about on the sand in a widely scattered group, as if placed to illustrate the solar system. They barely moved, or only moved if another moved. Venus crouched, looking at his toes. Uranus lifted his arms to his head, walked two paces to one side. Neptune hugged himself. Then almost all of them at once stooped slightly, as if a passing wind had brushed their backs. It was impossible to see if some signal may have been given. They seemed to have settled to these new positions wearily, as if they could barely give the matter their full attention. Nothing else happened. Then Mars, as if suddenly galvanised by physical discomfort, like Uncle Alfred and the wasp, started to stamp gently on the ground with both feet, lifting his knees higher and higher, finally flailing his arms and almost collapsing, doubled over as if in pain. At this, Venus lifted his clasped hands and turned to look sharply towards the sea, where Pluto was suddenly running along the tideline, as if to chase a wave before it broke slightly into flower.

The figures sitting on the benches, and on the edge of the terrace, applauded.

This rigmarole seemed infinitely remote from David and the girls, even though in the midst of their chasing their eyes kept returning to it, a world of toys or ghosts. But eventually they were exhausted. Their laughter subsided, and they stopped for repairs. Marjorie had lost her hat. Jill, too sturdy or stubborn to be grasped round the middle and lifted off the ground, had been pulled by the belt of her raincoat instead, and its loop was broken. Phillie, small enough to be lifted, had learned to retaliate by kicking out vigorously, running her feet in the air, and had caught David on the knee. They attended to themselves, flushed and breathless, and then ate David's ginger biscuit.

When they set off again towards Seaton Hall, though it was with more purpose this time, it was with no real conviction that they would ever get there. The self-containment of the dunes, that equal contest of field and shore, valour of grass and thistle, fluidity of sand: all this was like a spell for involving them in its timeless performances. Their presence brought it to life, an animal spirit for which the wind had sculpted it. Ahead of them, the dead institution and the joyless minimal movements of the ghostly cricket taking place in its shadow seemed by contrast only a mockery of life.

But suddenly they had arrived. Voices reached them on the air. They could pick out colours, a striped chair, green rugs, invalid blue. Their stride soon closed the last yards between them and the terrace. They saw bandages, mufflers, dressing-gowns, the batsman running between the wickets at his ease, a pipe in his mouth.

Jill had been telling them about her father's work at Seaton Hall. She had obviously also been looking at the surgical textbooks in her father's study, so that Phillie and Marjorie, already excited by so much running about, were in a mood to be frightened. David, who had once shaken Burroughs by the hand, knew what to expect, but was still disturbed. It was ridiculous, he supposed, since many, if   123

JOHN FULLER

not most, of the servicemen they could see looked like any other hospital patients. But the girls were already giggling and letting out theatrical groans at the Frankenstein horrors that Jill was relating, when they were noticed by a group of servicemen on the terrace.

'What ho!' said one of them, turning with a smile.

Another, with a bandaged head, stood up.

'Where on earth did that little lot come from?' asked someone else.

Jill was stalking on with her chin up, like a secretary in her lunch-hour pursued by wolf-whistles. The others stumbled after her, smiling to each other at the enormity of it.

The one who had stood up came towards the railings as they passed. David noticed, with the sickness of inevitability, the half-swathed face, the bright patched look about the eye, the stiffness in the area of the mouth like an expression pulled for shaving, the sharp edge of wig. It was Burroughs. His voice followed them questioningly, thin tortured syllables projected into the air from a barely moving mouth like a ventriloquist's.

The girls ran, screaming and laughing towards the car park at the side of the building. David could hear Jill's clear little voice announce busily: 'Yes, that's Daddy's Riley,' as though the car's identity or security had been the sole object of their single-minded dash.

What had Burroughs said? David was only about ten yards from the railings which separated them, and from which the airman looked down at him, but he could not understand. He had not yet slowed his pace, but he could hardly now pretend not to have heard. What could the airman want from him? What sign could he give of comradeship or reassurance? Later he was to reflect that it might have been Phillie's father standing there, and she would have been no less frightened. It might have been his own father. It might have been Jacko. Yes, that would be frightening, more frightening. It was the transformation that disturbed him. It was like somebody not yet born.

Again that thin voice, half dispersed by the wind! It was like the Witch's voice when they shouted at her, asking the time: 'Six o'clock!' An automatic voice, vague, distracted, saying anything for the sake of it. But there was purpose in the pilot's voice, and puzzlement. He was standing at the railings, with his arm raised and extended towards David, asking something of him. What could it be? There was nothing that David could say to him. He hurried on after the girls, in shame, with half a smile as though at nothing much in particular.

He knew he was running away, but he also knew that the airman's challenge was like something that was being given to him that he couldn't refuse. It was something that he was going to have to live with. He could feel the airman's gaze on the back of his neck as he passed. It seemed to sweep up into his short hair like the barber's clippers. It entered his skull. He was changed.

Somewhere overhead there was an aeroplane. Its sound was complex: the loudest part of it, only intermittent, was a kind of rending, the sort of noise that clouds might make in their passage through the sky if clouds could speak; but at its core was a sullen growling, like that of a caged animal.

12

By May there were a thousand Lancasters over Cologne, and Sylvia brought her baby boy back from hospital. Once that had happened David knew for certain that he had grown up. He couldn't have explained it, because it might have meant admitting that in some funny way until there was a new baby in the house he himself was still a baby. He supposed that until he had come back to Viewforth Road after the Blitz, Jacko had still been the baby. It was David's arrival, then, that had so soon turned Jacko into a man, unlikely process as that had seemed. Now David was free. But free for what?

His father had no need to collect him now, even if his work on the Lancasters was finished. Where could he take him to? The question seemed to be the same one. There were no real points of departure. They simply returned you to where you had started from, as he had been returned to Viewforth Road where before the war he had once been a real baby; as at Bellside Landing they had turned back to town; as a launched aeroplane had eventually to land.

But the point was, he realised, that the future itself was a real and continuous departure. And you made it for yourself. Nobody made it for you.

126

Captain Heart put this point clearly to his men.

'You're on your own now, boys,' he said. 'It's every man for himself.'

And rank upon rank they pressed forward to cheer, and to take up their positions for the final assault. No one was pretending that it was going to be easy, especially for those whose heads were only made of matchsticks and plasticine, but the crucial spirit was there. The force for truth was at last equalled by the force of numbers. There was a Lancaster for everyone, including the turkey.

In the stillness of the night, David discovered the secret attic above the attic. He had never before thought to climb above the grandfather clock, because that was not only outside his bedroom, but half-a-dozen steps downwards on the half-landing. But of course, if you worked it out, that had to be where the entrance was, because the ceiling was flat there, not sloping. And sure enough, there was a loft trap-door above the clock.

The baby had stopped crying hours ago. The house was quiet. The clock's slow tick was at once encouraging and admonitory, with a soporific regularity like the passes of a hypnotist. It did not count a particular number of seconds, but was irregular, like the pulse of a living thing. Once David had laced on his plimsolls for a better grip and mounted by way of the open clock door and the nearby banister on to the cornice of the clock, the tick, now below him, seemed infinitely distant. Being above it was like being outside its control, like being outside time altogether. The trap-door opened easily with a little push, like the lid of the cocoa tin. The hatchway was an inviting dark square.

The discovery of this space, linking all the houses at last, was the creation of a stage for enacting rites of passage. In the Borneo long-house, birth was remembered by

127

wriggling through the legs of the assembled families. At the other end was the enlightenment, the reward. What could that be? There was surely a way down at the other end, too. There was surely a different descent to the alley, perhaps to the mysterious green gate, or very likely to a different alley, a different way out of Viewforth Road. Could there be a way that he had never taken? It would be like having always taken the false turning in a maze, the pencil faltering through habit over the tracks it had already made.

This theatre in the eaves would bring great knowledge. It would contain all the forgotten lives and wisdom of the inhabitants of the street. The higher he could climb, the more of it he would find. They were simply waiting for him to find it. And everywhere boys like him were climbing with new-found dexterity, from door knobs to the tops of doors, on to wardrobe tops and picture rails, higher and higher, through lofts and hatches, up dead service-lifts into walled-up rooms and up old fireplaces, a thousand boys climbing up vents and chimneys, even though the ranges below were still alight, with night-time kettles simmering, on and on upwards, amid sparks, old cupboards glowing, the fire having taken a deep hold in forgotten shafts, but safely contained in the core of the immense timbers, on and on upwards, a thousand boys climbing, hair glowing, a determination in their eyes that could not be put out, climbing out into the night, a thousand burning boys.